theRoute

"Absolutely delightful! *The Route* shows all the depth and talent of Sears' previously published masterpieces in a witty, fun-filled romp full of warmth and humor. This is a book to read in one sitting—and then run out to buy for all your friends!"

—⸙ Kerry Blair

"*Sweet. Charming. Touching. Endearing.* These are just a few words I can think of to describe *The Route* by beloved author Gale Sears. I immediately fell in love with Carol and the other wonderful characters in this book who bring a rich layering of personalities, life stories, and backgrounds. When the book ends, your heart will be full but you will be left wanting more. Absolutely wonderful book."

—⸙ Michele Ashman Bell

"Filled with compassion, humor, and wisdom, *The Route* is a soul-pleasing feast to be savored by women of all ages, seasons, and circumstances. This is a narrative of lessons learned and hearts explored—it is at once poignant and tender, funny and feisty. Gale Sears again demonstrates her versatility as a best-selling author."

—⸙ Shauna Humphreys

"In her book *The Route,* Gale Sears demonstrates an uncanny ability to show the extraordinary in ordinary lives. . . . Her first-person narrative captures a depth of compassion that warms the heart and motivates a more active reaching out to those around us, especially the elderly. She weaves warm wisdom into her story in a way that leaves the reader feeling a deeper understanding of life's ups and downs. Yet Gale does it all in the structure of a captivating story so homey, so down-to-earth that it could happen to anyone, anyplace. And after you've read it, you feel it has happened to you."

—⸙ Darla Isackson

theRoute
Gale Sears

I dedicate this book to those who light a candle by giving of their time and hearts in volunteer efforts.

Walnut Springs Press, LLC
110 South 800 West
Brigham City, Utah 84302
http://walnutspringspress.blogspot.com

Copyright © 2009 by Gale Sears

All rights reserved. This book, or parts thereof, may not be reproduced in any form without permission.
ISBN: 978-1-93521-724-4

Acknowledgements

My great thanks to the tender people on the route that inspired this book, to the workers at the senior centers, to the meals-on-wheels coordinators, and to my trainer.

Also thanks to Linda Prince, my great editor, who loved and supported this book from her first reading of it, and to Amy Orton, Jack-of-all-trades at Leatherwood Press, whose instruction in "modern" technology and communication is slowly sinking in.

My final thanks goes to my ever-encouraging husband, George. He's a keeper.

Author's Note

The Route is a novel based on actual people and mostly actual occurrences that I experienced during a two-year space of time as a Meals-on-Wheels volunteer. The names used for the "characters" in the book were actual names of my clients, although I scrambled some of them to protect the innocent, appease the ornery, and satisfy the shy.

Cast of Characters

Goldie: the sunshine lady

LaRue: the cranky woman

Mary: the comic in thick glasses

Elaine: the recluse

Bea: the elegant owner of antiques

Olea: the wheelchair sweetheart

Maxine: the graceful missing person

Ladora: the dime-store aficionado

Lucille/Betty: mother and daughter duo

Joyce: GI Jane

Viola: the ornery stylista of the Airstream

Tom: the Last Emperor of China

Russell: Santa Claus

Althia: the voracious reader

Elsie: the lost and lovely one

PROLOGUE

Hi, I'm Carol. I'm a middle-aged woman with three grown children (chronologically, anyway) who are out of the house, which means I can tack empty nester onto my title: middle-aged woman, empty nester, college graduate, and wife to Bob. I'm also in charge of teaching Sunday lessons to the young women in our church. (It's like herding cats).

I can sew, but I can't bake. (I hear my mother's voice: "Carol when you say *can't* it simply means *won't*, so then of course you don't.") Does your mom speak inside your head? I lost my mom to cancer about three years ago. That's an odd way of saying she died, isn't it? I mean, it's like she was on a hike out in the wilderness, and cancer was some sort of ineffectual guide that got her lost in the woods, and if I were any sort of Girl Scout I should be able to find her again.

I love shoes, and traveling, and dogs, and I know I'm rambling, but I'm uneasy about getting to my point. In fact, I'm finding it difficult to just plop it down on the paper and share it with you, because it's all about—ah, Carol, just spit it out!—getting old and, well, dying.

Death and taxes, as my father often said, are the two things in life of which we can be sure. You see, my dad was a tax consultant and he loved to tease his moaning clients with that rosy sentiment. As a little girl I thought it was funny, but now I pay taxes, and every year as I step closer to the Grim Reaper, the humor of it fades. I never thought I'd be fifty, but that inevitable age has descended on me with condolences and jokes from my friends and family. It's only fair—I sent most of them sympathy cards on their half centuries.

Fifty makes you think. Thirty makes you morose, and forty makes you panic, but fifty makes you think. Half a century, and what is my life? Does it resemble anything I dreamed at sixteen, or expected at twenty, or hoped at twenty-five? What am I doing on this planet? I realize that spiritual geniuses have been pondering and answering that particular question (or one similar to it) for thousands of years, but for me enlightenment is a grueling process. This mental weightlifting prompted consideration of possible ways to boost my spiritual awareness. I considered enrolling in a college course entitled Comparative World Religions, but I chickened out when I thought about sitting in class with all those young people—guys with finely tuned philosophical minds, and brilliant girls with exposed, tan tummies. Then I thought of climbing to the top of a high mountain in Tibet to consult a wise man, but I like vacations where there's indoor plumbing and vegetation. Since I already attended church, I thought perhaps I could pay closer attention. Maybe I'd been missing a great fundamental truth. Well, come to find out, I had been missing something. *Lose yourself!* What a knock on the head. If you lose yourself, you'll find yourself. Sounds kind of Zen, doesn't it?

Actually, as I evaluate the world from my fifty-something suburban- housewife sensibility, I think service is in short supply pretty much everywhere. Oh, sure, there's the occasional philanthropist building schools in poor neighborhoods, or the big-hearted doctor working in a clinic in Asia, or church groups working to help the poor and the needy, but what about the rest of us? To heck with the rest of us! I can only control me, so what about me? I mean, it's all well and good to ponder life's great mysteries, but isn't it better to get out there and do something?

After this grueling mental workout, I went to the grocery store to look for chocolate, and I saw a notice for an organization needing volunteers. I took it as a sign! That afternoon I enlisted in the program and became a delivery person, delivering meals to stay-at-home folks. Every Thursday, my route brought me briefly into the world of some very fascinating people—people older than myself, some way older, people whose background, decisions, and experiences created the fiber of their personalities. Their diverse lives taught me much about the different roads we travel to get to that final destination, and the following pages are a synopsis of the journey.

I thought I'd share it with you.

Yes, indeed—death, taxes, and so much more.

CHAPTER 1

I Learn the Route

Valerie from the main office accompanies me on my first Thursday to make introductions and show me the ropes. She is an intelligent young woman, a college student, energetically pursuing a master's degree in social work.

"All the directions you need are on these papers," she says brightly. "They're stapled together, see? It'll be in the food bag, right on top. Names, addresses, special instructions—like if they don't get milk or if their meal comes cut up or puréed. Stuff like that."

"Okay," I answer, trying to sneak a peek at the names on the list.

Valerie pulls her puffy red hair into a high ponytail. "You should have your deliveries done no later than about 12:30. Is that a problem?"

"Not at all."

"See, some of 'em eat their lunch early, like 11 a.m., and they get worried if the food's not there by noon or so."

"Gotcha."

"Your route's gonna change. I mean, not a lot, but sometimes somebody goes into a rest home for a while, or the hospital. Sometimes a new person gets put on the list temporarily. Stuff like that."

"Okay." I smile at her clever-minded efficiency and junior

high slang.

"Oh, you have an SUV. Great! That'll make it easy. Careful when you lift the cooler and hot bag—sometimes they're heavy."

"Oh! Oh, yeah, you're right. Thanks." I bend my knees and heft.

"So, are you ready?"

"I am."

She jumps into the passenger's seat. "You drive, and I'll tell you which way to go."

"Perfect."

"Today you have twelve people—seven in an apartment complex, and the others in homes or trailers."

It's a misty November morning, and I turn on the wipers to clear the windshield. Our first stop is Goldie's. Goldie lives by herself in her own home. It's a large home in an older established neighborhood, and, in its prime, it was probably a show place.

Valerie points to the home on the west side of the street. "See, there's Goldie standing at the window. Cute, isn't she?" Valerie burbles. "I feel like a giant around her. I swear she's only five feet tall."

Actually Valerie is five feet three inches, and Goldie's probably a petite size 4. At size 12, I'm a giant.

"If she's not at the window, just knock loudly and wait until she answers the door. She likes to do it herself, but sometimes it takes her a while."

The tiny woman from the window opens the door and beams at us. "Oh, look! I have two ladies today!" Goldie's hair is stunning white, her eyes alert, and her smile infectious.

Valerie opens the screen door. "Hi, Goldie! We have your meal."

"Wonderful! Come in, come in."

"Goldie, this is Carol, and she'll be delivering every Thursday."

I extend my hand and she takes it. "Hi, Goldie. It's nice to meet you."

"It's nice to meet you too. Was it Hazel?"

"Carol."

"Oh, Carol. Good. Well, come to the kitchen and set the food on the table. What did you bring today?"

Valerie hands me the papers. "The menu's on the last page."

I flip through the pages. "Ah, looks like barbeque chicken, new potatoes, cherry crisp, and green salad."

Goldie winks at me. "Well, don't they send the most delightful lunches? Thank you so much for bringing it."

Goldie is sunshine. Her mother probably took one look at her as a newborn and came up with her name straight away.

Valerie finishes setting out the food. "Okay then, Miss Goldie, Carol and I are off to our next drop."

"Here, let me walk you to the door." She touches my hand. "And I'll see you next Thursday."

"You will."

"You're a sweet girl."

I feel like I'm twelve—a good twelve, a twelve full of possibilities. We leave Goldie's house and move down the brick path to the SUV.

"Now watch as we go to drive away," Valerie says.

I glance back at Goldie's house and spot her standing at the window. When she sees me look, her face lights up and she waves.

Valerie chuckles. "From what I understand, she waves like that to all the drivers."

I wave and pull away from the curb. This is fun. I'm going to like doing this.

Our next stop is the Maple Leaf Apartments. We load up two plastic carry baskets with seven lunches, then head quickly for the entrance. A sharp wind blows across the parking lot, whipping the information papers out of the basket. Valerie runs after them as I pick up the lunches. Boy, these things are heavy!

Once we enter the hallway, it takes a minute for my eyes to adjust to the dimness. "Are some of the lights out?"

"No, I think the management just wants to save money," Valerie answers.

As we move along the hall I notice signs hanging over the door handles—signs that read I'M OKAY. The residents must have to hang the placards out every morning so the office staff can tell who's made it through the night. It's odd to think of a time when I'd have to put out a sign announcing my condition. Now, if I wake up not feeling well, I know my faithful spouse will take one look and say, "Man, honey, what's the matter with you? You look awful." And he'll bring me juice before he heads off to work. The mostly women who occupy this apartment building must miss a personal someone to keep watch on how they're doing. It's such a little thing, but I hadn't given it much thought.

Valerie stops to knock at room 113.

"What?" The voice on the other side of the door is harsh.

Valerie whispers, "This is LaRue. She's sort of cranky. Don't let her scare you."

Scare me? I've raised teenagers.

Valerie knocks again.

"Who is it?"

"We have your lunch, LaRue."

"Well, come in. You know to come in."

Valerie opens the door confidently. "Good morning, LaRue!"

La Rue sits on the couch watching a soap opera. "Morning? What time is it?"

"Eleven forty-five."

"Hardly morning."

"LaRue, this is Carol. She'll be delivering your meals on Thursday."

I move towards her. "Hi, LaRue, I'm glad to—"

"Don't step on that!"

I jump. "On what?"

"That plastic hose. That goes to my oxygen."

"Oh, I'm sorry. I—"

"What are we eating today? Not chicken, I hope. I hate chicken."

Valerie bravely steps in. "Barbecued chicken, new potatoes, and cherry crisp."

"I like potatoes."

"I know you do. Here's your milk."

"Don't like milk."

"I know, but it's good for your bones."

"Bones schmones."

LaRue's face looks like one of those little shrunken apple people that the kids make at Halloween. If she were wearing a peasant dress and shawl instead of a purple bathrobe, she would be the perfect model.

Valerie catches my eye and nods towards the door. "Well, we're off, LaRue. Carol will see you next Thursday."

"If I'm not dead."

We step into the hallway of the apartment building and I find my voice. "I hope I didn't damage anything."

"You mean the oxygen hose? No. You didn't even step on it. LaRue's just . . . well, she's just . . ."

"Cranky?"

"Yep."

I suppose I'd be cranky too if I hated chicken and milk, and had to be on oxygen.

We venture on down the hallway and come to a door with a sign that says, I DON'T DO MORNINGS!

Valerie chuckles. "Mary. She's a character." She knocks loudly on the door, but there's no answer. She knocks again. Nothing. She turns to me. "Sometimes they have doctor's appointments."

I put my ear to the door, noticing that Mary's I'M OKAY sign is out. It sounds like there's movement in the apartment. "I think she's in there. Could she have fallen or something?"

"It's possible."

Another loud knock. The neighbor across the hall opens her door to glare at us, but Valerie is fearless. "Excuse me. Do you know if Mary's in?"

"What? Mary who?" The woman croaks out.

The Route

I'm wondering if this woman is related to LaRue. The woman slams her door as Valerie knocks one more time.

"If they don't answer after three or four knocks, you can check to see if the door's unlocked." Valerie tries the handle and the door opens. She steps inside. "Mary? It's—" She nearly collides with a large woman in a brown pantsuit.

"Yikes! Who's there? Oh, my! You scared the wits outta me!"

"Oh, Mary, sorry," Valerie says. "We knocked, but . . ."

"I didn't hear. I was in the bathroom, fan on and everything. Just finished. Come on in. You're that lunch lady."

"That's right. I'm the trainer, and this is Carol. She's going to have the route on Thursdays."

"Great, terrific. Good to see ya."

See me? I wonder if that's possible. The lenses of Mary's glasses must be three-quarters of an inch thick. I smile broadly. Maybe she can see my teeth.

"Just set everything on that little desk by my chair, okay? I'll be over there in a minute. It takes me awhile."

Valerie clears a space and turns to instruct me. "Now, Mary's meal is marked NO DAIRY. Be sure she gets that one, and juice."

"Oh, mercy, don't give me milk!" Mary exclaims as she hobbles towards her chair. "My stomach would be a rootin' tootin' Wild West show."

I smile at Mary's spunky manner, wishing she'd been my best friend in junior high school. I probably would have breezed through braces and pimples with the comical Mary by my side.

Mary lowers herself slowly into her green velour recliner.

"Oh, dang! I forgot my fork and spoon. Did I swear? Sorry about that. It just takes me so long to get someplace."

"Don't worry," Valerie chirps, "we'll get them for you." She goes to the tiny kitchen and brings back the utensils. "So, are you all set?"

"All set, thanks."

I smile at Mary, but she's already at work, pulling the cellophane wrapper from her meal. "I'll see you next Thursday," I say with a wave.

"I'll be here."

We step into the hallway. "Is she always so positive?"

Valerie nods. "From what the other drivers say, she is."

Now, Elaine is a different story. She comes to answer the door on the first knock, opening the portal just wide enough for us to hand her the food, then firmly closes the door with her foot.

We don't see Bea. There's a note on her door that says she's at the hairdresser, and to please leave her lunch in the fridge.

Apartment 139 is Olea. Her apartment is in the section of the building where walkers and wheelchairs are a way of life. Olea gets one of the meals where all the food is cut into small pieces. We enter the apartment quietly, and Valerie tells me about undoing the lid of Olea's meal tray and opening her milk carton. Olea sits in her wheelchair waiting for the lunch. She is so twisted by arthritis that her neck is bent into a curve that forces her head down. Her wrists are bent at odd angles, and the joints in her hands are so swollen and crooked as to render them almost useless.

Valerie bends over as she places the food on a tray attached to Olea's chair. Her voice is gentle. "Hi, Olea, here's your lunch." She places a straw into the milk carton. "Can I help you with your spoon?"

"Yes, please."

Valerie places a special spoon into Olea's hand. "Olea."

"Yes."

"This is Carol. She'll be coming on Thursday."

I realize I've been standing frozen in my place. I bend down. "Hi, Olea." Despite myself, my voice is low and husky.

She lifts her chin slightly. The skin on her face is pale and transparent, her eyes a dull gray. She smiles and nods her head. "Would you do me a favor?"

"Of course."

"Move me away from the window. It's a little drafty."

There is an ache in my chest that makes it hard to breathe. "Is that better?"

"Yes, thank you."

Valerie pats her hand. "What time's your aide coming today?"

"Two o'clock."

"Good. Is it still Margaret?"

"Yes. Two years now."

Valerie looks over at me. "Margaret is so cool."

Olea smiles and points at me. "What was her name again?"

"Carol. She'll be coming every Thursday."

"That will be nice." With effort Olea works her spoon into the cherry crisp. I look up at Valerie and realize the unguarded emotion registered on my face. I move quickly to pick up the food basket, then exit into the hallway. My hand brushes against the I'M OKAY sign on Olea's door handle. I wonder if there's a flip side that says I'M TERRIBLE, I NEED HELP!

Valerie joins me in the hall. "Are you all right? Her circumstance is a tough one."

"Doesn't she need someone with her twenty-four hours a day?"

"She's able to do some stuff for herself. Takes her a long time, but she does it. Then Margaret comes almost every day. Margaret will be the one to say when she needs to go into another type of facility."

"What about her family?"

We move down the hall. "She has a daughter that lives in town, and one in Arizona. The one in town can't take her, and the one in Arizona won't."

"Won't?"

Valerie shakes her head. "It happens all the time."

I feel like there are rocks in my stomach.

I don't register much about my first meeting with Maxine, except that her apartment is sparkling clean and classical music is playing—something from Vivaldi's *Four Seasons*. At this point all I want to do is get out of the apartment building into the cold air. Maybe I made a mistake. Maybe I could volunteer someplace else—be a teacher's aide for cute little kindergarteners. Why am I volunteering at all? I could join a bridge club or learn to play golf. Yeah, I've put in twenty-five years raising our kids. It's time to take it easy. I trudge down the hall after Valerie, trying to convince myself that I want to be a lady of leisure instead of a woman of emotional substance.

Our final stop in the building is Ladora. She greets us warmly at the door and brings us into her dollar-store-decorated wonderland. She has the rhinestone-encrusted kitty clock with the tail that swings back and forth, a counter full of Chia pets (all thriving), and a three-feet-tall ceramic cactus in perpetual bloom. On her walls hang pictures of the Bavarian Alps, Waikiki, and the Washington Monument. I wonder if they're places she's actually been, or just places she's dreamed about going.

"Is it lunchtime already?" Ladora questions. "Where did the morning go? I haven't even finished my crossword." She stares at me the whole time she's talking. "I don't know you. Are you new?"

"Ladora, this is Carol. She'll come every Thursday."

Ladora holds out her hand for a hardy handshake. "Well, that'll be nice."

"I like your apartment," I say, meaning it.

"Yeah? Me too. My daughter says it's junk—wants to throw everything out and redo. She's an architect."

"Do you see her a lot?"

Ladora snorts. "Almost every day."

"That's so great!" I reply a bit too enthusiastically.

Ladora gives me a funny look. "Great? Well, I guess. Sometimes she can be a pain in the butt—bossy, you know."

Valerie comes to stand beside us. "Ladora, I've left your meal on the table."

"Good place for it. I'll eat and finish my crossword."

I hand her the newspaper. "I'll see you on Thursday, Ladora."

"Adios, senoritas."

I feel a weight lifting off my chest. I don't even mind being back out in the dim hallway with the brown commercial carpet.

"So, that's the Maple Leaf lot. What do you think?" Valerie asks.

Think? I think it's going to take me days to process all this new information. "I liked the cactus." Belatedly, I realize it's a dumb thing to say, but Valerie just smiles and nods as we move off to the SUV.

A light rain blurs the windshield and I turn on the wipers.

"Go left on Connell, right next to that antique store. Just over the train tracks, north side of the street."

We pull up in front of a tiny, faded house with stained curtains in the windows.

"Now, Lucille and her daughter live on the left side of the duplex," Valerie points out.

Duplex? How is that possible? The house itself would be considered small for a single-family dwelling.

"Lucille doesn't leave the house much, and she doesn't get much help. The daughter's name is Betty. She needs constant care."

I turn off the engine. "How old is she?"

"Betty? About thirty-five, I think. She has some sort of rare sickness, kind of like cerebral palsy." Valerie jumps out of the truck. "Now, Lucille has asked that we bring her a newspaper. Don't forget it, okay?"

"No. No, of course not."

As we move up the pitted walkway, past the dead grass, my heart is pounding. I don't think I can handle this. We're at the door with its chipped white paint, and Valerie is knocking. I concentrate on the patter of rain on my umbrella. Maybe I can pretend to hear my cell phone ringing in the car. Valerie knocks again, and dogs start barking from somewhere at the back of the house. Maybe I can say I'm afraid of dogs. Just as I'm backing down the crumbled concrete steps, the door opens.

"Yeah?"

The smell that escapes the house is putrid—old food and unwashed bodies.

Valerie smiles. "Hi, Lucille. We brought lunch."

Lucille is a fierce-looking woman, about five feet five inches tall and at least 230 lbs. Her gray hair is pulled into a braid that looks as if it was created days ago. She pushes errant strands of hair away from her face, then reaches to open the screen door. I smile as I stare past her into a living room, which is not a living room. An old hospital bed occupies most of the small space, and propped up on the grimy pillows, in a semi-sitting position, is Betty. She is watching television. Well, she's staring at the movement on the screen. Her lips are pursed, and her arms and hands jerk involuntarily. Her hair is greasy, and her nightgown is stained with food. As I look down at the newspaper in my hand, I hear Valerie introducing me to Lucille.

". . . and she'll be here every Thursday."

I look up quickly. "Hi, Lucille. Here's your paper."

"Thanks." Her voice sounds like a meat grinder.

Valerie is handing over the food. Lucille takes it and places it on a small bed that's been shoved against the wall. Valerie and I are guards passing food between the bars of a prison. My hands have gone ice cold. I look down at my shoes and hear the door close.

"Valerie, I'm sorry, I . . ."

Valerie takes my arm. "It's okay. You did fine. That's

probably the hardest one on this route. Really, you did fine. Let's head to Joyce's. It's just down one block and over one block."

I'm glad Valerie doesn't talk on the way to our next stop. Down one block, over one block. I can do this.

"That's Joyce's house. That big two-story."

Joyce's house is lovely: clean white paint, brown shutters, fenced yard, and well-kept grass (even in November). We place her meal in the plastic basket and Valerie leads out.

"Joyce is very bright. She was a military nurse in World War II, but she doesn't talk about it much."

I'm envisioning one of the Andrews Sisters in a crisp military uniform and bright red lipstick.

"She likes you to ring the doorbell and then just walk in. She's usually sitting back in her kitchen, and she's too frail to come to the door. She's got emphysema." Valerie rings the bell and calls out as she walks in. "Hello, Joyce! It's Valerie."

From the back of the house comes a small, rasping whisper. "Come in. I'm in the kitchen."

It's a man's voice, and I try to picture the woman creating such a sound. The house smells of cigarette smoke—years of cigarette smoke.

"Well, hello, Miss Valerie from the main office. I haven't seen you in a month!"

Joyce is a featherweight, a one-time classic beauty fitted over with a mask of premature wrinkles. She has intense blue eyes and ivory hair. "And who is your friend?"

"Joyce, this is Carol."

"How do you do, Carol? Joining the ranks?"

"Yes, ma'am. I'll be coming on Thursdays."

The Route

"Same day as my aide. You may bump into each other."

It's hard to get used to someone so petite having the gravelly voice of a truck driver—a truck driver with emphysema.

"So, Miss Valerie, what's keeping you busy? Still working on your master's degree?"

"I am. Another semester or two and I'll be done."

"Feather in your cap. And you, Miss Carol? How do you spend your hours?"

My mind races. Part-time work, full-time mothering, church activity, shopping, cooking, cleaning, appointments, feeding the dog, cleaning the bird's cage, reading . . . the list goes on and on, but all that comes out of my mouth is, "Well, I do a lot of laundry."

Joyce laughs and lights a cigarette. "Ah, yes. A woman's life could be so splendid if it wasn't for laundry."

"And toilets," I add.

Joyce laughs through a cough. "How right you are, Miss Carol." It is some time before she can talk again. "I'll look forward to seeing you every Thursday."

"It'll be great to come."

"And I'll see you in another month or so, Miss Valerie?"

Valerie nods. "Whenever there's somebody new on the route."

Joyce points a finger at her. "Now remember, young lady, all social work without socializing makes for a very dull life."

Valerie giggles. "I'm dating. I am."

"One or many?"

"Many."

"Good for you. Date and compare."

25

Valerie blushes. "Come on, Carol. Let's get outta here before she starts asking me if they're sexy or not."

Joyce smiles. "Well, are they?"

"Joyce! You're terrible!"

"When your only companions are books, you grasp at straws."

The doorbell rings.

"Yeah, right. Your aide's here, and if I remember correctly, he's a hunk."

"He is. You girls vamoose so I can have him to myself."

The door opens and a warm male voice calls out, "Joyce, it's Alex."

Joyce snuffs her cigarette and motions us out with a smile.

"See you next Thursday, Joyce."

We pass by Alex in the living room, and, wow, he is gorgeous! Both Valerie and I gibber something to him as we head for the front door. Outside, we stop to gulp down cold air.

"Wow!" Valerie says, looking a little starry-eyed.

"Wow. That's just what I was thinking," I stammer.

Valerie stumbles down several steps. "I forgot how hunky he is. If you time it right, you can bump into him every Thursday."

We giggle like schoolgirls. I'm a bit past fifty, and I'm behaving like a fourteen-year-old. Actually, it's one of the things I like most about being a woman—the ability to carry all my previous ages around with me and unpack them at the appropriate times. I also like how quickly women can bond with each other. I'm already concerned how Valerie will do with her grad work, hopeful that Ladora will be able to keep her dime-store decor, and anguished about Olea's daughters—will they ever rally around? The deep caring that women do is a blessing and a burden. I sigh and attempt to convince myself that I don't need to take on the problems of the world.

Valerie suddenly checks her watch. "Yikes! We'd better get a move on, or Viola will chew off our ears!"

"What?"

"Viola does not like you to be late," Valerie informs me as she sprints towards the truck.

I race after her. I hate having my ears chewed off. The last time it happened was Mrs. Panatoni—fifth grade. I'd been fed up with Matt Fisher teasing me, so I'd pushed him off the monkey bars. Matt had a big mouth, but his body was sort of wimpy. When Mrs. Panatoni kept me after school, I thought she would make me write a hundred times "I will not push Matt Fisher off the monkey bars." Huh! I only wish writing had been my punishment, because my actual sentence was much worse. Mrs. P. chewed my ears off for fifteen minutes. She didn't yell, but instead used all these big words and a horrible disappointed voice that made my insides feel like cold worms. Oh, no! I was not about to get another ear chewing! Even at fifty, the thought made me shiver.

We travel a maze of small streets until we come to a trailer park. From the age of most of the trailers, the park was probably established in the early 1970's.

Valerie points at the street sign. "Viola's is on the corner of Carnation Lane. Number 147. Right around here. Oops! There she is out on her front stoop waiting for us."

"Are we really going to get our ears chewed off?" I ask.

"Probably."

As we approach, I squint to get a better look at my punisher. I smile. This little woman does not look fierce. She is ninety lbs and five feet tall. She has on a cotton floral duster, cinched around the waist with what looks to be a man's tie. She stands out on the stoop of her sleek, silver Airstream, a showy travel trailer that gave up traveling long ago. For some reason, someone's painted the bottom half a dull buff color. It looks like an Airstream stuck in a sand dune. I pull into a parking space beside Viola's trailer.

"She doesn't look so tough. I bet we can take her."

Valerie raises her eyebrows. "Hmm."

I jump out of the SUV and wave.

"Oh, oh, oh. Well, there you are. There you are," the little woman calls.

I smile as I load her lunch into the basket. She has the same sweet voice of my kindergarten teacher, Miss Greenough. This is going to be a piece of cake.

She pulls her tea-towel shawl tighter around her boney shoulders. "I thought you'd forgotten all about me. I called the office to see where you were. I was just ready to chew on some old crackers. I'm near starved to death."

"Morning, Viola," Valerie answers despondently.

"Well, now, it isn't morning, is it? Not morning at all." The tone of Viola's voice is still sweet like Miss Greenough's, but for some reason I feel like toilet paper on the bottom of someone's shoe.

Valerie straightens her back. "Sorry we're a little late, Viola. This is Carol, and she's learning the route, so it took us a little longer."

Oh, sure, blame it on me.

As we approach the front stoop, a small, black poodle rushes at us, barking and snarling. Well, snarling with no teeth. This dog could be the poster child of the "all bark and no bite" contingent.

"Buffy! Get back there, you rotten dog! I'll smack you silly!" I look up to Viola's face to see if some Dr. Jekyll thing is going on. She smiles. "That's my pooch. He's as old as the hills."

I glance at Buffy's frosted eyeballs and mangy coat and think, *Methuselah dog.*

"Just put my lunch here on the milk box," Viola commands. "I'm just so glad you finally showed up. I was getting very hungry."

"I'll be earlier next Thursday," I respond with a smile.

"Will you?" she asks, giving me a cold glare.

I shiver and nod, the smile freezing and falling off my face.

"Well, that'll be nice, won't it? Maybe then I won't have to starve while I'm waiting."

I am determined not to be intimidated. "Are you sure you don't want me to take this food inside for you?" I ask, moving to open the door.

"No! You stay out of my house!" Viola growls. When I look at her quickly to see if she's pulled a kitchen knife out of her duster pocket, she smiles. "No, thank you. You don't need to take anything inside for me. I didn't ask you to, did I? I don't know that you'd find your way around in there."

Buffy cowers behind Viola, whimpering. I know how he feels. I'm thinking of *The Wizard of Oz*, the part where the witch is sweetly saying, "Poppies . . . poppies . . ." as she's about to poison Dorothy and her friends to death.

"Off you get so I can have my lunch, now." Viola's voice brings me back to the front stoop. "The food's probably cold, isn't it? But that's all right. Don't you two give it a second thought. I guess it's better than crackers." She disappears into her trailer with Buffy trailing.

"Quick, let's get out of here," Valerie whispers.

I glance at my food companion, who looks to be on the verge of a giggle fit. "Is she always like that?" I ask as we head for the sanctuary of my vehicle.

"From what the drivers say, she is. And she's always calling the office. It doesn't matter if you're two minutes late or twenty minutes late."

"She calls the office?"

"Every day," Valerie laughs. "Oh, man. You should have seen your face when she yelled at you about going into her trailer."

I try to shake off the feelings of the past ten minutes. Maybe I'll start the route with Viola and end with sweet Goldie waving from her window.

As Valerie flips through the instruction papers, she looks like she's attempting to regain her composure and get back to business. "So, now we head back to the senior center to drop off all the stuff. Put a check by every name on the list where we took a meal, and sign your name on this line. See, here on the last page."

"What if someone isn't home, like Bea?"

"Good question. Mark 'not home' by their name, and if you

can't leave the meal, then give it to someone else. Lucille and Betty can usually use it. Next time, if you have any questions or comments, there's a place where you can write them. There's also a phone number on the front where you can call about any problems or concerns."

I envision myself filling reams of paper with questions and comments, and spilling my guts every Thursday afternoon to some poor yokel at the main office. I open my mouth to share this, but what comes out is, "Oh, it all seems pretty straightforward, pretty doable." *Does Valerie believe a word of this tripe?* I wonder. Out of the corner of my eye, I see her eyebrows go up, and I decide to come clean. "Actually, I think most of it's going to be okay, but some of it is . . . well . . . hard. I mean, do any of the drivers get used to it?"

"Nope."

"No?"

"Sometimes there are really tough cases. If you're a caring person, it hurts."

We're quiet the rest of the way back to the senior center. I fill out the forms and unload the food containers, then shake hands with Valerie.

"You're going to be great!" she says, smiling brightly. "We're so glad you're on the team. Do you have any questions?"

I look at her blankly. "I don't think so."

"Well, if you do, just call me, okay?"

"I will."

We shake hands again, and she's out the door to her VW Bug. I watch as she tosses her bag into the backseat, reties her mop of red hair, and climbs into the driver's seat. She's probably thinking of grabbing a taco for lunch and heading to the library for some study time, her life in front of her.

As I drive home, I think of Joyce, and Olea, and Mary. I also consider that a week from now I'll be maneuvering the route solo. A mantra shuffles through my head. *I can do this. I can do this. I can do this.* I also ponder that my small route is repeated a hundred times throughout the city. All those lives I'd thought nothing about. Where have I been for fifty years?

CHAPTER 2

Solo

I'm at the senior center early for my first solo Thursday. It's 10:55 a.m. on a glorious November day, with a Maxfield Parrish blue sky, and cold air that dictates mittens, not gloves. I'm feeling nervous. The papers from the main office contain all the information I need to get around, but following written directions has never been one of my strengths. My older daughter has always had to help me translate those big mall directories, then point me in the right direction. Well, who can tell which way is north when you're inside a building?

As I check the list of people on my route today, I realize I'm worried about saying something stupid, or stepping on LaRue's oxygen tube, or accidentally giving milk to Mary. I take a deep breath. *I can do this. I can do this. I can do this.*

The lunch today is meat loaf, mashed potatoes, green beans, and an oatmeal cookie. My stomach growls and I remember that I didn't eat breakfast. Great. I can see myself halfway through the route, pulled off to the side of the road, wolfing down meat loaf as I dream of my school-lunch days. What would Valerie think of me then?

I load the containers into the SUV and head off. My first stop is Goldie's. I realize I'm looking forward to seeing her, and I wonder if she'll be standing at her window. Probably not, as I'm a good twenty minutes early. I think I remember the name of her street, but I check the office papers to be certain. Knowing me, I could be wandering back roads for days.

As I drive through the neighborhood, I notice an absence of childish paraphernalia in the yards: no bikes or basketball standards or chalk hopscotch on the sidewalk. It's a neighborhood that has raised its children and sent them off into the world to be artists or plumbers or CPAs. Some of the kids would marry and have families, and some wouldn't. Trials and achievements would be encountered along the way, and while some of the youngsters would grow up to enlighten the world, others would struggle with basic concepts like choice and consequence, or right and wrong. I can relate. Our oldest, brilliant daughter (the one good at directions) somehow went astray in her choice of a husband. Bob and I tried to warn her, but at twenty-three she was sure she could make a logical, informed decision. Our middle child, also a bright, happy girl, is at college trying to decide if she would rather be a vet tech or a model. Our son has demons to fight, and not just the ones he encounters in computer games.

I pull up in front of Goldie's home and notice a car in the driveway. *How nice, she has a visitor.* I put her lunch in the basket and head for the front door, checking the list to see if I'm supposed to knock or ring the doorbell. The instructions say to knock loudly, so I do. I hear footsteps approaching from inside the house—heavy footsteps that certainly don't belong to Goldie. The door is pulled open, and I put on my smiling greeter face. In front of me stands a tall, lanky man in faded jeans and a long-sleeved black t-shirt. His gray hair settles on his shoulders. His face does not smile back at me.

"Hi! I'm Carol with Goldie's meal. Is she here?" Only then do I see her standing behind him in the hallway. The lanky man opens the screen door and I hurry past, headed for the kitchen. "Hi, Goldie, it's Carol." She smiles, and for a moment it's just the two of us. Goldie is dressed in navy blue slacks, a white blouse, a red and blue plaid vest, and a red hat. She looks très chic. "Goldie, you look wonderful."

"Do I? Thank you. Robert's taking me to lunch. Robert, this is my friend Carol. She brings my lunch every Thursday. Carol, this is my boy, Robert."

Robert extends his hand. "I'm glad to meet you."

"Glad to meet you too, Robert."

"It's nice of you to bring my mom's lunch." I'm surprised at the tenderness in his voice. "She says the food is real tasty."

Goldie gently touches my arm. "Can we just put it in the refrigerator, and I'll have it for dinner?"

"Of course." I follow her to the refrigerator, berating myself for all my petty thoughts. I had been wondering how someone like Robert could know someone like Goldie, and imagining the offensive and wicked tattoos he must be hiding under that long-sleeved shirt. *Prejudging. I need to do something about that character flaw, or I definitely won't be going to the good place.*

"So, where are you going for lunch?" I ask with a smile.

"Probably Chinese," Robert answers. "Mom loves Chinese."

Goldie smiles up at him. "Miso soup and egg foo yung."

Robert puts a hand on her shoulder. "And don't forget the fortune cookies."

Goldie laughs. "Robert always gets me extra cookies so I

can choose which fortune I like best."

I smile at the incongruous pair, trying to imagine them sharing stories over ham fried rice. "Well, you two have a great afternoon, and I'll see you next Thursday."

Goldie walks me to the door. "Oh my, it's beautiful today, isn't it?"

"It is."

She pats me on the back. "Drive carefully."

I unlock my vehicle door, put the basket on the seat beside me, and start the engine. I ease the SUV into drive, then glance over to Goldie's house. There she is, standing in the doorway. When I smile at her, she waves. I wave back. Could anyone not love her?

I'm so lost in thoughts of what it would have been like growing up in Goldie's house that I miss the road for the Maple Leaf apartments and have to backtrack. Good thing I gave myself extra time. I find a parking place and begin loading my baskets with lunches and cookies and drinks. An old man creeps by on his electric cart, giving me a stern look.

"You can't sell nothing here," he barks.

"I know. I'm just dropping off food."

"Oh. Oh, well, that's all right, then. Don't forget to lock your car."

Hmm. I wonder if he was a policeman in his younger years. I recheck the list to make sure I have the same people that Valerie and I went to last week. Yep. No add-ons. I heft the baskets. *I can do this. I can do this. I can do this.*

Apartment 113. LaRue. I knock loudly.

"Come in."

The Route

That does not sound like LaRue's voice. I enter cautiously, looking for oxygen tubes. A voice calls from the bathroom area.

"Who is it?"

"It's Carol. I have LaRue's lunch."

"I'm Barbara, her aide. She's getting her hair washed. Just set the stuff on the counter, okay?"

"You're early!" LaRue calls from the bathroom. Her voice makes me jump.

"I know. Yeah, you're right. I am. I thought I'd start out a little early this time in case I got lost or anything—first time out solo and all. I'm not too great when it comes to directions, and I can get turned around, so I thought I'd give myself a little extra time." I know I'm rambling, but I can't stop myself. "Yeah, first time on the route alone, I thought it would be better if I started out, you know—early."

"What'd they send?"

"Meat loaf and mashed potatoes!" It's weird yelling at a bathroom.

"Well, that's not too bad."

"No, it should be good. Well, I left everything just here on the counter. So . . . okay then . . . I'm off to my next stop. See ya next time. Have a . . . good day." I'm out the door before the end of my sentence. What a chicken I am! I resolve not to let LaRue's harshness intimidate me in the future. I wonder if she's always been a cranky person, or if that arrived with her illness—and the oxygen tank.

I've met some people who are in the prime of their lives—healthy, financially stable, and intelligent—but who are emotionally greedy. People who don't share genuine warmth of feeling with anyone. I shudder to think what kind of old people they're going to be, especially if they have a run in with illness and oxygen tanks.

I knock loudly on Mary's door and am immediately invited in.

I hear her voice from the front room. "Oh, just keep on whining, as if that's gonna solve your problems."

I move into the front room to see if Mary's talking to me. Actually, she's conversing with a television newsman, snorting at the events going on in the state and making editorial comments about the local political situation. She looks up as I enter, her eyes large behind the thick lenses of her glasses.

"Can you believe this? Wants a recount on the recount. Guess his mama didn't teach him to be a good loser."

"I know, it's crazy, isn't it?"

She looks at me sternly. "Did you vote?"

"I did."

"People think their vote doesn't count? H—E—double toothpicks! Let somebody tell me their vote doesn't count and I'll punch 'em in the nose!" She mutes the television. "Sorry 'bout that. It just stirs me up." She leans closer to me. "Now, you're new from last week, right?"

"Right. I'm—"

"Wait, wait! Don't tell me. You're Pearl."

"Carol."

"Oh, right. Carol. Carol. Well, just put my lunch on my little side table here. I already have my silverware."

"So, I take it you voted."

"Oh, you bet! They have a bus you can call. Picks you up

at your front door and takes you right to the voting place. I haven't missed a vote in some sixty years. Can't wait for the next Presidential race. I ain't votin' for anyone without values, that's for sure."

My mind races back through the Presidents: FDR, Truman, Eisenhower, Kennedy, Nixon, Ford, Carter, Reagan, Bush, Clinton, Bush, and now Obama. I wonder which ones Mary voted for, and which against. I have a feeling Slick Willy was not her candidate.

"Now that my grandson's got me one of them dish things, I'm as happy as a clam. What's for lunch?"

"Meat loaf, mashed potatoes, green beans . . ."

"And a cookie! Good stuff."

"And apple juice."

"Yep. No milk for me. Crazy mixed-up insides. I used to drink milk by the truckload. You have a dish?"

"Excuse me?"

"TV dish."

"No. Cable."

"Too bad. I get about three hundred channels!"

"Wow!"

"Don't need that many, but I sure do like the news and sports stations and the History Channel. Lots of movies, too."

I'm trying to imagine what she actually sees with her thick glasses. The inquisitive part of me wants to ask her, but the mother inside my head says, "It's very rude to ask personal questions."

Mary fishes the remote control out of the side of her green velour recliner and waves it in the air. "Aren't these the best things?"

"They are."

"You remember when we didn't have these?"

"Of course."

"What a pain in the butt. Have to get up to change the channel."

"Well, there weren't that many channels."

She chuckles. "That's true."

I can tell Mary's anxious to get back to her news commentary, so I pick up my basket and head for the door. "I'll see you next Thursday."

She waves a spoon in my direction. "Good enough! Keep your fingers crossed that all these shenanigans are over by then."

"I'll do it."

Out in the hall, I have to laugh. I imagine Mary in the polling booth, leaning close to the touch screen and poking her choices with determination.

Mary's enthusiasm makes me realize that politics, travel, and learning of all kinds are activities I can choose to keep current as I age. Of course, all that depends on the status of my mental and physical health, some of which is uncertain fog in a crystal ball, but there are things I can influence. I vow to be more consistent with exercise, and the eating of veggies, and not consuming pastries and ice cream except on very special occasions. (Of course, I've been known to invent special occasions in a pinch.) I also vow to spend more time with my friends, indulging in madcap adventures, wearing purple, and laughing until our sides ache.

I knock on Bea's door.

"Come in. Come in. The door's open."

I step inside. The room is dim. "Hello? I'm here with your lunch."

A lamp is turned on, and I move into the front room. Bea sits in a lovely wing-back chair with her feet propped up on a small stool; over her lap lays a beautiful knitted blanket in tones of dusty rose. She is an elegant woman with salon-perfect chestnut hair done up in a French twist. Her skin is pale, but she wears a bit of blush and a soft, rosy lip color.

She sits straighter in her chair. "I was just taking a little nap."

"Oh, I'm sorry to wake you."

"Not at all. I need to have my lunch. Are you a substitute?"

"No. I'm Carol. I'll be coming every Thursday."

"How nice. I'm Bea. I just have my lunch here on my table."

I place the food tray on a lovely lace tablecloth.

"Would you mind slipping one of those plastic mats under the food? They're not very attractive, but they work."

As I rearrange things on the table, I find it hard to imagine Bea ever slopping food anywhere. My impression of her is of finishing schools, and lessons on proper etiquette from the age of six. As I get out her carton of milk, I feel as though I should pour it into a crystal goblet. I pause to take in the surroundings, noticing that Bea's small living space is filled with exquisite antiques. Everywhere there is dark mahogany, silver, and crystal. I'm no expert, but I'd bet little Bea could make a killing on *Antiques Roadshow*.

"Your home is beautiful."

"How sweet of you to say so. These are just a few things. Most of my pieces are in my daughter's home. She takes very good care of them."

"I bet each piece has a story."

She looks around at her treasures. "Yes, they do. Do you collect?"

I think of my department-store furnishings. "No, but I love to walk through antique shops. I wish I knew more about it."

"My husband Randolph and I loved collecting." She hands me a small, framed picture. "That was taken of the two of us in Amsterdam. Our sixtieth anniversary. This tablecloth came from there."

"It's beautiful."

"Randy passed away just two years after that trip. Five years ago now."

"You must miss him."

"I do."

I see Bea's thoughts drift to another time and place, and I feel like an intruder on her cherished memories. "Well, I'd better be off to my next stop."

She looks at me and smiles. "Oh, of course. Thank you for coming, Carol, and thank you for the visit."

Visit? I was with her for all of three minutes.

"I'll see you next Thursday, Bea."

"That will be lovely."

As I move off, I see her reach for her cookie. *Ah, she's a woman after my own heart—start with dessert.*

The Route

Out in the hall I try to calculate her age. Now, say she was married at twenty . . . married sixty years . . . that would be eighty . . . add another seven . . . eighty-seven! Impossible! I'd been thinking she was in her early seventies, but, of course, that wasn't possible either.

I'm still trying to accept Bea's age when I arrive in front of Elaine's residence. I knock and immediately the door opens, making me jump. Man! In order to open the door that quickly she had to be standing right by it, peering through the peephole, waiting. It's creepy—like one of those trap-door spiders. I'm trying to catch my breath when out comes her hand, motioning for the food. Huh! I'll show her! Instead of handing her the food, I hand her my hand.

"Hi, Elaine. I'm Carol. I'm going to be bringing your lunch every Thursday."

She snatches back her extremity. "Did you wash?"

I'm a tad offended. "I did."

"Give me my lunch," she growls.

I hand over the goods and she closes the door abruptly. Well, at least I heard her voice.

I move to Olea's apartment, mentally going over the things I need to do for her: take the lid off the meal, make sure everything's cut into small pieces, open her milk carton, put in the straw, hand her the special spoon, bend low so she can see me. Suddenly I feel queasy. I stop at her door to make sure the I'M OKAY sign is out. After taking a couple of deep breaths, I knock. *I can do this. I can do this. I can do this.* There's no answer from inside, so I knock again. The door opens and I'm looking at a very tall woman in hospital scrubs. She smiles broadly and the world lights up.

"Hi, I'm Margaret, Olea's aide. Come in. You're a new one."

"I'm Carol. I come on Thursdays."

"Glad to meet ya." She moves to Olea and gently touches her arm. "Hey, sweetie, your lunch is here. Do you feel like eating?"

Olea shakes her head. Margaret pats her shoulder and moves back to me. "Let's just put it in the fridge. She's having a bad day."

Margaret opens the door and I put in the meal. I notice that there are only a couple other items in the refrigerator.

"She doesn't eat very much, does she?"

"No. It's hard for her. She'll be going into a facility soon."

"Will that be good?"

"Oh, sure. Someone there twenty-four hours a day." Margaret closes the refrigerator door. "It'll be strange. I've been with her almost every day for two years."

Looking up at Margaret's face, I see deep compassion. My idea of angels has always been slim, airy women in gauze dresses. From now on, they're going to look a lot like Margaret—tall, sturdy women in hospital scrubs.

As I prepare to leave, I just can't stop myself from asking, "She has two daughters, doesn't she?"

"She does."

Margaret and I stand whispering in the kitchen.

"Well . . . don't they . . . I mean . . . can't they help?"

"Oh, they could help, sure. They don't want to. They're just waiting around to fight over the inheritance."

I wasn't expecting such a straightforward answer. "You're not joking, are you?"

"Nope. It happens all the time. Olea will be okay. I got her some financial counseling about a year ago. Tied up most of her money so she can go into a real nice facility for as long as she needs. One daughter threatened to sue me."

I catch myself staring. "Unbelievable! Good thing Olea has you."

"Well, nobody deserves to be mistreated."

"I don't know. It seems like her daughters could use a good swift kick."

Margaret laughs. "Oh, honey, they're gonna get theirs someday."

"You think so?"

"I know so."

"Margaret?" Olea's voice comes weak and frightened from the front room. Margaret moves to her immediately. "I'm right here, sweetie."

"I don't feel well."

"I know. It's the new pain medication. Let's get you to bed, okay?" Margaret's voice and manner are so soothing.

I set down my basket. "Is there anything I can do?"

Margaret is undoing the brakes on the wheelchair. "I've got it covered, Carol, but thank you for asking. Olea will see you next Thursday."

Olea glances in my direction, and her right hand comes up in a feeble wave. My throat tightens. I croak out some sort of good-bye and move out into the hallway. I am so angry I want to kick something. Selfish daughters! Actually, that's the pair

I'd like to kick. I see myself in these big, steel-toed boots, and the daughters have bare legs—skinny, bare legs. *Okay, okay, calm down. Olea has Margaret. Margaret cares about her. I can do this.* I find myself marching to my next stop. I'm not feeling very Zen.

When I arrive at Maxine's door, I stop and take a couple of deep breaths. Then I see a note on the door explaining that she's gone to a movie with a friend, and asking me to please leave her meal with her neighbor across the hall. *Okay, I can do this.* I tap on the neighbor's door, wait, then knock again.

"Hey! What do you want?" A voice snaps from behind me in the hallway, and I jump.

"Do you live here?" I point at the door.

The woman nods. "What's it to you? You're not supposed to be snooping around, you know. We have very strict security here."

"Maxine said to leave her lunch with you."

"Again? Where is she this time?"

"Movie."

"Gadabout." She opens her door. "Hand it over." I do. "Anything else?"

"No."

"Okay, then." The door shuts with a snap.

Hmm. Efficient.

As I move off to Ladora's place, a savory smell comes wafting out of one of the apartments. Yum. Spicy, like something Mexican. My stomach grumbles. I find myself thinking of the thousands and thousands of meals cooked by the women in this apartment building—of all the families fed and sent on their way—and I'm staggered by the impact of that one small, consistent act of service. It's not anything I considered much growing up. I mean, we had to eat, and somehow food just showed up on the table and we ate it. Who cared about or appreciated all the time it took to gather recipes, figure out menus, shop for the food, store the food, cook the meals, and clean up afterward. The only time we kids were aware of food issues was when something was missing. *"What'd ya mean we don't have ketchup? How am I gonna eat this hamburger without ketchup?"* There's that saying, "The hand that rocks the cradle rules the world"? Well, I think it's also, "The hand that makes the lasagna or pot roast or tuna casserole surprise, rules the world."

I'm wondering what kind of cooks the women on my route used to be.

As I approach Ladora's door, I see that she has decorated it with a bright yellow sign that reads ENTER AT YOUR OWN RISK. I bet her architect daughter is having a fit over that.

I knock, and soon Ladora opens the door.

"Hello there! Come in. My stomach's been growling for the past fifteen minutes."

"Oh, sorry. Am I late?"

"Oh, no, no, no. It's just that when my neighbor starts cooking, I turn into one of them Pavlov dogs."

"I know! When I walked by her apartment, my stomach started talking to me like crazy."

Ladora maneuvers past her ever-blooming cactus and heads towards the table. "She has me over for dinner once in a while, and man, is she a good cook. Very spicy, though. I don't suppose we're having tacos?"

"Meat loaf."

She looks disappointed. "Ah, well. I guess they figure it's not safe to give us old guys spicy food. Mashed potatoes?"

"Yep. Green beans. Oatmeal cookie."

Ladora rubs her hands together and smiles. "I guess I'll just have to make do."

I chuckle and attempt to set down her food. The table is crowded with a mishmash of items: newspapers, mail, prescription bottles, knick-knacks, hand lotion, a harmonica (I wonder when she plays and if she's any good), a box of crackers, and a can of fake cheese. I hesitate a moment and finally set the tray on top of the newspapers.

"Oops! Let me grab my crossword." She slides the top newspaper out and sits down at the table.

"Do you still cook, Ladora?"

She gives me a quizzical smile. "Only if it's an absolute emergency. I was never very good at it. Plain, simple stuff. Now, I have a daughter who's a smarty-pants cook. Fancy stuff."

"Is that the one who's the architect?"

"Yeah. Did I tell you about her?"

"Only that she was an architect."

"Her name's Kristine. She's my baby—thirty-eight, and still my baby. I had her when I was thirty-seven. She was a surprise. She has two older brothers, one who is forty-nine and one who is fifty-one. Yep. She cooks French stuff."

I recheck Ladora's food items. "I think you're all set."

"Oh, I'm as happy as a plow horse in the winter."

"Okay, then. See you next Thursday."

"Adios!"

As I move out into the spicy hallway, I'm feeling pretty good. I check my watch. Hey! I may even be early at Viola's. No ear chewing today. The sun is bright as I come out of the dim hallway. I squint my way to the SUV and climb in. Next stop, Lucille and Betty. *I can do this.*

I get a little lost wending my way to their tiny duplex, but I've given myself plenty of extra time, so I'm not concerned when I drive up in front of the house and see Lucille standing at the front door. Unlike Goldie, she is not smiling or waving.

As I'm loading their lunches into the basket, I realize there's no newspaper. The meal distribution place forgot to include the newspaper, and I'm the one who has to answer for it. I glance over at Lucille, who is still not smiling. I swallow and put on my cheery face. Today it's my oh-please-don't-be-mad-at-me phony cheery face.

"Hi, Lucille!" The screen door comes open. "It's mashed potatoes and meat loaf today!" I'm handing over the food. "Green beans." No response. "And . . . your milk, and oatmeal cookies. Yum!"

"Where's the paper?"

"They forgot to send the paper today."

"Are you kiddin'?" she says with scowl.

"Sorry."

"It's all I have to do in the afternoon. What's wrong with you stupid people?"

"I'm sorry . . . I . . . I'll call the office and make sure they don't forget again."

"Stupid government agencies."

I want to remind her about the meat loaf, mashed potatoes,

and oatmeal cookies, but I only apologize again, as she shuts the door in my face. I stand there for a second, blinking at the chipped white paint. I guess I should be angry, but what I feel instead is a deep sadness. I'd hate it if the happiness of my day hinged on a newspaper. What kind of life does someone have whose contentment depends on headlines, comics, and the sports page? Getting into the SUV, I head in the opposite direction of Joyce's and Viola's. I know I'm going to be late at Viola's and will get a wicked ear chewing, but I don't care. I drive to the 7-11, buy a paper, drive back to Lucille's, and knock on her door. Shortly, she pulls the door open and stands glaring down at me. "What?"

I smile and lie. "Actually, they did send a paper. It was down under the last of the meals, so I missed it."

She slowly opens the screen door and I hand her the paper. She stares at it, then at me. "You came back to bring me this?" I nod. "That was nice. Thanks."

Again the door closes in my face, much more gently this time. Such a simple thing. My dad used to say, "A gate swings on a very small hinge." Fifty-plus years old and it finally dawns on me exactly what that means.

I knock on Joyce's door and walk in, bumping smack-dab into Alex, who was clearly coming to open the door for me.

"Yikes, I'm sorry! I thought the paper said to knock and come in."

Alex is laughing. "Yeah, that's right. I was just on my way out to pick up Joyce from her doctor's appointment. Are you okay?" He's still laughing.

"Yeah, I'm fine. Listen, can you just take this stuff for me and put it in the refrigerator? I'm late for my last stop, and the lady gets kind of cranky."

He gives me a wonderful, warm smile. "Can do."

I yank my eyes away from his attractive face, hand over Joyce's lunch, then race back to my vehicle.

Alex calls after me. "Hey, slow down. Maybe Miss Cranky Woman needs to learn patience."

"Huh! Fat lot you know!"

He laughs.

I'm praying that Viola will go easy on me because it's my first time out solo, but I doubt it. I drive carefully and make it to her trailer in record time. She isn't standing out on her front stoop. That's a good sign! I load the basket and head for her Airstream. As I step up onto the stoop, I hear her pitiful pooch yowling from inside. I knock, expecting the dog to launch itself into a rash of barking, but it just continues to yowl. I hear footsteps coming slowly to the door.

"Hi, Viola." I'm shocked by her ghastly appearance. Leave aside the purple and pink aloha muumuu that she's tied around the waist with a man's brown and orange tie, and the bright pink tennis shoes, the most worrisome feature is her face. Her skin is sallow, and dark smudges sit under her bloodshot eyes.

Her voice cracks with exhaustion. "Oh, oh, oh. My pooch. My poor old pooch. I don't know what's wrong with him."

"Is he sick?"

"I don't know. He started whining in the middle of the night. He won't stop. He's making me nuts. Could you look at him?"

"Me? Well, I'm not a vet."

"I know, but maybe you can see something."

I'd only glanced at the mutt the last time I was here, and all I could remember was old and mangy.

Viola snarls, "Buffy! Buffy, shut up and come here!"

"Are you sure he can get up?"

She ignores me. "Come here, crazy dog!"

Buffy comes slowly to the door of the trailer. I sit down on the step and coax him to me. He creeps forward with his tail between his legs. His coat is matted, his eyes goopy, and he smells bad. I see a big bulge on the side of his jaw. Immediately I think tumor. Raising kids, I've had plenty of pet experience—birds, gerbils, and hamsters—and along with these little friends come tumors.

"Viola, he has a bulge on the side of his jaw."

"Do you think that's it?"

"Probably. He needs to go to the vet."

"He does?"

"Yes. Can you get him there?"

"My niece could come pick him up."

"I'd have her do that. Today. He's in a lot of pain." I absently scratch the top of Buffy's head, while he shakes like a Tahitian dancer.

"Oh, my poor old pooch. My, my, my. Buffy! Get in there, now! Get inside!" The little poodle reluctantly leaves the scratching and crawls back into the trailer.

I stand up, trying hard not to touch my hand to any other part of my body. Good thing the meal staff always sends along antibacterial wipes. I look at Viola's tired face. "Can you call your niece right away?"

The Route

"I can. Thanks for looking at him. My lunch is probably cold, isn't it?"

I set the things on the milk box. "Still seems a little warm."

"I can always have dry old crackers. Well, thank you so much for coming. I was just half starved to death, and worn out with that stupid dog. I'll go eat my lunch and call my niece." As she shuts the trailer door, Buffy begins yowling again, and I hear Viola yell at him.

Poor old pooch. I stow the food baskets in the back of the SUV and use up a week's worth of antibacterial wipes.

When I arrive at the senior center, I pull under the covered driveway, put the vehicle in park, and turn off the engine. I've made it through my first solo Thursday. I've made it! I didn't get lost, or forget anyone, or step on anyone's oxygen tube. I'm actually a bit amazed. Getting down to paperwork, I check off the meals delivered, make a note about no newspaper, and sign my name. I drop the bags in the designated place in the lobby, and stop by the bathroom to wash my hands. Two ladies from the afternoon bridge club are chatting away about the big bingo—potluck night coming up, and I think how much fun Mary would have at that shindig. If she could see the numbers on her card, I'm sure she'd be the life of the party.

CHAPTER 3

Detours

Thursdays came and went quickly, and Valerie was right—my route did change. The names were becoming people to me, and I always felt a shock when I'd check my list and find a name missing. There was never any explanation as to why the person was gone; her place on the page was just squeezed out by the person above and the person below. If the name was at the bottom of the page, it just dropped off into nothingness. I'd always call the office for information, usually talking to James or Corina.

"Hi, James, this is Carol."

"Hi, Carol."

"Somebody is . . ."

"Missing on your route?"

"Yep. Would you check and see the reason?"

"Sure."

Most of the time it was a doctor's appointment, or an overnight visit with family members. But sometimes it was a trip to the hospital, or stays at a rehab facility.

"I didn't have Joyce today."

"Ah . . . Joyce . . . Joyce . . ." I can hear James ruffling through papers. "Joyce has gone into the hospital."

"Oh? Which one?"

"St. Mark's. Went in on Monday."

"Do you know what for?"

"Nope. Sorry." James hangs up, and I sit staring at the phone. I hate to call hospitals. Even if the news they give you isn't tragic, there is usually some sort of pain or challenge involved.

I call St. Mark's and give them Joyce's name. As I wait for the nurse to get back to me, my mind jumps around as to what might have happened: her emphysema might have clamped down on her, she could have had a stroke, or maybe she's had an operation of some sort.

"Hello. This is Nurse Kimball. You were waiting for information on Joyce?"

"Yes." I take a breath.

"Are you a family member?"

"Friend." I don't know if Joyce would consider me that, but I figure it would be too hard to explain the nature of our relationship.

"She's recovering from surgery. She's in room 402, but won't be able to take phone calls for two or three days."

"What type of surgery was it?"

"I'm not able to give out specific information. She can have visitors tomorrow."

"So, she's doing okay?"

"She's resting comfortably."

I doubt that. I've never known anyone who's "rested comfortably" in a hospital—poolside in Maui, yes, hospital, no.

"Any idea when she might be released?"

A hesitation. "Perhaps Saturday."

"Well, thank you. I'm . . ."

"You're welcome." There's a click and the conversation is over.

I love nurses. They're so efficient. Nurse Kimball's voice had been soft and reassuring, and I'm sure she would have stayed on the line for a nice chat if she'd had the time. I could see her in my mind's eye, charging down the beige hallway to answer a patient's impatient buzzer.

Surgery. Resting comfortably. Okay, if Joyce is released on Saturday, I'll probably see her next week.

The same Thursday, as I'm dealing with concerns about Joyce, I get a shock at LaRue's apartment. I knock on the door and brace myself for the her harsh response. Nothing. I knock again and hear a faint mewling sound from inside the apartment. I open the door.

"LaRue?" I hear a soft whine again. "LaRue, are you in here?" I move into the front room and find her lying on her couch in a fetal position.

Now, there's a very good reason I never became a nurse or an EMT, and that's because I panic in a crisis, and the manifestation of that panic is not hysteria or fainting, but freezing. I just sort of stand rooted in one spot with my imagination flying around inside my skull at a hundred miles an hour. *Is she having a stroke? Is her oxygen tube blocked? Was she watching one of her soaps and something tragic happened? Did her dog die? Oh, she doesn't have a dog. Maybe I should call 9 . . . 9 . . . my brain is numb!*

"Who is it?"

I'm jolted into reality. "It's me, LaRue. It's Carol. Are you okay?" *Stupid question.* "Can I do anything?" I set down my baskets and move to the couch.

Her mouth opens and closes several times but no words come out, only small croaking sounds. I check the oxygen tube for kinks. Seems fine.

"Should I call someone?"

She shakes her head no. "My daughter... my daughter..." Tears wash down her cheeks. "Coming to take me to the... rest home." New tears. "I won't come out of there."

I can't think of anything to say. I sit down at the end of the couch and put my hand on her feet; they're ice cold. I grab a small throw blanket from the back of the couch and put it over them.

One of her soaps occupies the TV screen. Some handsome stud in Levis and a t-shirt has his arms wrapped around a lovely brunette in a wedding gown. The volume on the television is muted, but I can imagine the conversation.

"*Oh, Tony, please don't do this. It's my wedding day.*"

"*But, it should be* our *wedding day.*" He pulls her close to him. "*I need you Stephanie. I need you.*"

He begins passionately kissing her neck, and shoulders, and ... whoa! This is daytime television? I suddenly realize I've lost all sense of my surroundings. I grab the remote and click off the TV. I breathe slowly to calm my pulse rate.

I feel guilty for abandoning LaRue, but when I turn to talk to her, she's fallen asleep. She looks small and defenseless, her puffy hands unable to hold back the forces shaping the end of her life. Congestive heart failure. I hate this! I'd much rather have the cranky, unpleasant woman fighting through each day—each hour.

The front door opens. "Mom?" A middle-aged woman

wearing a gray coat and brown boots comes into the room. She sees me and her eyes narrow. "Who are you?"

I stand up sheepishly.

"Well?"

I feel like I'm answering LaRue again. For some reason, it makes me feel better. "I'm Carol. I deliver lunch."

"Oh. Well, don't leave anything today. In fact, tell your office not to deliver any more meals here."

"Well, I think you have to call with a cancellation. Do you have the number?"

She glares at me. "No."

"I'll write it down for you." After finding a napkin and a pencil, I write down the number. "Here you go."

She snatches the napkin away from me. "Great, one more thing to take care of."

"I'm sorry your mom has to go into a rest home."

"Sorry? What do you know about it?"

"Nothing. It's just that I . . ."

"Don't you have meals to deliver?"

I nod and turn to leave. I want to say good-bye. I want to wish LaRue well, but she's sleeping, and her daughter stands guard like a pit bull. I know I won't see LaRue again. I take one last look at her sleeping on the couch, pick up my baskets, and move out into the hallway. As I stop for a moment to fight back tears, I watch a silver-haired woman in a lime green pantsuit putting a sign up on her door. I amble over to see what it says.

OLD AGE IS NOT FOR WIMPS.

I smile.

"Like my sign?" she asks with a wink.

"It's wonderful."

"It's true," she says brightly.

I nod. It is true.

❧

Joyce is home the next Thursday, but she's in bed, looking gray and feeble. She smiles and tries unsuccessfully to talk to me. She's not up to eating anything, so I put her meal in the refrigerator and bring her a glass of water. I help her sit up, holding the glass for her as she takes a few sips. This small effort wears her out, and as soon as she lies back on her pillow, she closes her eyes. I miss her calling out my name. I miss her caustic jokes and rude comments about local political leaders. Joyce, with her truck driver's voice, has become one of the highlights of the Thursday route. I walk out of the dim house into the sunshine and meet Alex coming up the walkway.

"Hi, Alex!"

"Hi, lunch lady."

How cute is he? "She's not up."

"No? Well, it looks like I might have to get tough with her." He smiles and I feel my knees go a little wobbly.

"Did she have throat surgery? When I asked her how she was doing, she just put her hand up to her throat and shook her head."

"Yeah. This is surgery number two."

"Two?"

"Yep. Throat and mouth cancer. All those years of smoking."

"And she still smokes?"

"Yep. She has emphysema and throat cancer, but she's

addicted. Of course, the tobacco industry is going to tell you that nicotine's not addictive." A cold anger comes into Alex's voice. "They're not going to accept any responsibility for the hundreds of thousands of people they kill every year. The CEOs are cruel, evil people. I wish every single tobacco company president would die of emphysema or throat cancer or lung cancer." He sets down his backpack and stoops to tie his shoe. "Sorry. Didn't mean to go off like that. It's just that Joyce is going to die a terrible death."

I feel tightness in my chest. "Is she?"

Alex stands up and looks right into my eyes. "Yeah, she is. Slow suffocation." He shakes his head. "If you tried breathing through one of those little cocktail straws, you'd get an idea of what it's like. That's emphysema."

My imagination picks up on this immediately, and tears jump into my eyes.

"Oh, sorry," Alex says softly, taking my arm in his hand. "I get a little intense about this stuff."

"It's okay. You have a right. Why doesn't the government do more?"

"Huh! Good question. If there was any other big company killing so many people, their product would be off the shelf in a second—no lobbyists, no deals, no argument."

We stand silent for a moment in the sunshine. I take a deep breath and think about lilacs blooming in a month.

Alex picks up his bag. "You okay?" I nod. "Well, I'd better go see if I can get the duchess up and walking." He heads for the house.

My voice follows him. "You're great, Alex."

He smiles. "Hey, just doing my job, like you, lunch lady."
I look down at my volunteer badge. I remember a time I thought this was only about delivering lunches.

Oh my gosh! A jolt of fear races up my spine. I still have Viola, and I am so late! I run for the SUV. *Ear chewing!* I have been so careful about being on time. I can shave off some minutes if the traffic and stoplights will cooperate. No such luck. I take a deep breath. *Okay, I can handle this.* I'll just ignore her double-sided remarks and churlish innuendo. I'll block out her poor-pitiful-me act. So what if she has to eat crackers for a few minutes until her hot lunch shows up?

I'm feeling somewhat confident about how I'm going to handle the little woman, until Carnation Lane comes into view, and I feel myself wilting. Maybe the Airstream won't be there. Maybe Viola got a wild hankering for the open road and took off for Las Vegas. Hmm. Again, no such luck. Viola stands out on her stoop wearing a frown and a bright orange duster. Like the captain on the deck of a ship, her hand shadows her eyes as she peers out to sea. The dread pirate Viola. She spies my SUV and glares.

I hear her sweet little voice saying, "One cannonball broadside should finish her off!"

I pull into the driveway and give myself a pep talk. *Be strong. What can she do, get you fired?*

Viola is still frowning as I move up to the stoop. I decide to take the offensive. "Lunchtime! Today you have two lunches!"

"Two?" The scowl disappears.

"Yep. One of my ladies wasn't home, so I thought you

might like the extra meal."

"I am very hungry. I had to wait for you a long time."

"Now, I hope you didn't eat crackers and ruin your appetite, because I have breaded chicken patty with mashed potatoes and gravy, mixed veggies, and chocolate pudding."

Viola is mute. I smile at her pleasantly.

"Two chocolate puddings?" she asks, her face almost kind.

"Yep." I start to pile the stuff on top of her old milk box. *That ought to keep her from yapping for a while.*

"That was nice of you to bring me two lunches. I get so hungry sometimes."

I look at the gaunt face, the orange duster cinched around the waist with a man's blue tie, and I feel like dog poo. Great. This is probably the only hot meal she gets all day. I'm thinking of kicking myself.

"Did you know that my old pooch died?"

"I did, Viola. About a month ago, wasn't it?"

"Is it that long? Oh, I miss my old pooch. He was making me nuts. My niece took him down to the vet, and he never came back. I'm sure they gassed him. Oh! I like your shoes! Where did you get those?"

I feel a bit off balance. "I don't remember—maybe Fashion Footwear."

"Oh, those are very nice shoes. I think my niece could go pick me up a pair."

"Well, I've had them about a year, so . . ."

"Is this all the food you brought me?"

"Yes, ma'am."

"Well, I'm gonna go eat now, so you can take off. Don't be

late next time. You're lucky I didn't call the office." She begins hauling food into the trailer.

"Okay, Viola. See ya." How can I be irritated with her? Maybe I'll end up alone in a trailer, wishing every day that somebody would bring me an extra chocolate pudding. It's like that Native American saying, "Don't judge anyone else until you've walked a mile in their orange duster."

CHAPTER 4

Potholes

Spring had arrived early, drying the soggy flower beds, softening the air, and putting most of the older people into much better moods than they'd been in during the dreary winter months. Of course, some seniors carried spring around with them, no matter what the meteorologist forecasted.

"Hi, Goldie!"

"Hello, my dear."

"Isn't it a beautiful day?"

"Just what I wished for."

I join her on her front porch. "Good wishing."

"Robert brought out the lawn chairs for me. He told me I was rushing things."

"Never! Did they see their shadow?"

"Who?"

"Your lawn chairs."

"I don't think so."

"Then spring is officially here."

"Wonderful." She laughs at my silly joke. How nice of her.

I notice that Goldie looks pale and seems a little tired. It's probably just from being out in the bright sun. She is dressed as dapper as ever in a pair of gray polyester pants, a white turtleneck, and a purple vest. What class to get up every morning, without prospect of going anywhere, and dress to the nines. I remember my Dad telling me that when he was a young man, men always wore a suit, tie, and hat when they went into town, and women wore dresses, hats, and gloves. It's evident that Goldie grew up in that same era of respect. I vow to wear my sloppy sweat outfit only when I'm exercising or having a bout with the flu.

"Where would you like your lunch?"

"Well, I'm not very hungry right now. Would you mind sticking it in the refrigerator, and I'll have it later?"

"Sure." She starts to get up. "Stay put. I can find my way."

I watch her melt gladly back into her chair as I head for the kitchen. Goldie's home is clean and calm. Her daughter-in-law comes in every other day to visit and tidy up. Actually it's an ex-daughter-in-law, but the bond these women have forged is stronger than any spousal parting of the ways. Goldie elicits loving kindness from people because she is loving and kind. I wish the truism *You get back what you give* was actually true. But all too often it doesn't seem to work out that way, especially when we see kind people receiving horrible treatment at the hands of miscreants, or despicable people prospering. Our hearts ache with the injustice. It's then I have to remember what Olea's aide, Margaret, said: "Oh, honey, they're gonna get theirs someday."

I don't know when someday is, or what the cosmic process of punishment will be, but isn't it interesting that in every metaphysical school of thought, there is a day of reckoning where our actions and thoughts are weighed and appropriate consequences given? A day when there will be no cover-ups, no taking of the fifth, no hiding, and no lawyers?

I come out onto the front porch and find Goldie snoozing. She wakes when the screen door shuts.

"Oh, I dozed off."

"You did."

"That sun feels so good."

"Well, you enjoy it." I move down the steps.

"Thank you, Carol, for my lunch."

"You're welcome. See you next Thursday."

I hop into my vehicle, stowing the basket on the passenger seat. I start the engine and turn to wave. Goldie's hand comes up for a small princess wave and then returns to her lap. I chuckle and make a mental note: *Execute princess waves when you're in your eighties. People will find them charming.*

I head to the Maple Leaf apartments, anxious to meet a new add-on. His name is Tom and he resides in apartment 133. Up until now I have had no men on my list, and I'm ready to be nosey and find out his circumstance.

There are far more women than men in senior apartments and care facilities. Now, my dad had a theory on this, and it was that women are tough on men and that's why the poor old guys go first. He'd laugh like crazy after making one of these "life observations," especially during my teen years when he saw how I reacted to his fake chauvinism. I remember a conversation we had years later when I was the matriarch of my own home, raising three kids and dealing with the difficult stuff of life. We were discussing the pros and cons of insurance policies.

"You know, you will probably outlive your husband," he said with a grin.

"Dad."

"Well, you will."

"I know, because I'm so tough on him he'll go first just to escape me."

He chuckled. "Gotcha on that one."

"Funny."

"And it's not because he's a couple of years older, either. If you were older, he'd still go first."

I remember scowling at him. "Of course. It's probably because I have the easier job—staying home taking care of the kids."

He shook his head. "Give me a briefcase or a backhoe any day. You'll outlive him because you're tough. Women in general—you're tough people."

"You believe that?"

"I know that. Look what you've had to go through with your youngest."

I was stunned. My dad had three daughters, and I'd always believed he felt cheated not having sons—that somehow he thought sons were better. Not so, apparently. From his simple comment, I realized he'd noted every one of my accomplishments, honored my battles with adversity, and cherished my strength. I was one of those tough people he admired, and even though I knew he'd continue to tease me about my feminine shortcomings, the edge was gone.

I pull into the Maple Leaf apartment building and marvel at the soft green of new leaves playing on the branches of every tree. Maybe everyone loves spring so much because of the increased oxygen.

I load the baskets with a supply of hunter's stew, green

salad, dinner rolls, tapioca pudding, and beverages, and head for apartment 133. I figure I'll start with Tom so I can spend a few minutes getting to know him.

The master sheet says to knock and then wait for him to call for you to come in. I follow the instructions.

"Oh! Come in! Come in!" The voice is oriental.

I open the door and pick up my baskets.

"Come in, please."

"Hi, Tom?" I move into the hallway.

"Yes, yes, come in." Tom puts down his newspaper and rises from a comfy-looking chair. He moves to meet me, smiling brightly. What a cute man! I know men don't find it flattering to be called cute, but there is no better term for Tom. Definitely cute. He stands about an inch shorter than me and is much slighter of build. It's like Viking Woman meets the Last Emperor.

"Hi, Tom. I'm Carol."

"Oh, yes. Good."

"I'll be coming every Thursday."

"Oh, Thursday. Good. Good."

I get the feeling he's not too comfortable with English.

"Where are you from originally?"

"Originally?"

"Where were you born?"

"Ah. China. Guess how old."

"How old you are?"

"Yes. Guess."

I look him over. "Seventy-five."

Tom laughs and his eyes sparkle. "Not good guess. Guess

again."
"Seventy-two."
"You going wrong way."
"Eighty."
"No." He's laughing again. "Ninety-three!"
"Get out of town! You are not ninety-three." I am genuinely flabbergasted. Sometimes I fudge a bit when seniors ask me to guess how old they are, especially the women. I'm not above playing into their flights of fancy, but I had truly calculated Tom's age to be between seventy-five and eighty.
"You don't believe."
"I don't. You're pulling my leg."
A spate of laughter. "I not pulling your leg. Ninety-three. Pretty good, huh? Very much health. I go doctor tomorrow for check."
"Are you driving?"
"Me?" He chuckles. "Oh, no. No. I not drive long time. Four, five years. My daughter, Phyllis, she drive."
"Well, don't let that doctor give you any trouble."
"Oh, no trouble."
"You're probably healthier than he is."
"Than doctor?"
"Sure."
"Maybe, maybe." Tom's eyes twinkle.
"So, I want a full report next Thursday."
"Okay, full report. You come every Thursday?"
"Yep."
"Okay, you Thursday girl."
I smile. "I'm very glad to meet you, Tom."

"Glad to meet you. Thank you for lunch."

"Have a good day." I pick up my baskets.

"Oh, I get door." Tom moves around to the side of me and opens the door.

"Thanks. See you next time."

"Okay. Next time."

The door closes behind me, and I stand for a moment in the hallway with a silly grin on my face. One of the apartment managers passes by.

"May I help you?"

"Huh?"

"Are you lost?"

"What? No. Oh, no. It's just that I . . . ninety-three. Can you believe it?" The woman scrutinizes my face as I ramble. "Oh, never mind. No, I'm fine. Just on my way to Mary's to drop off her lunch." I move quickly down the hallway, sure that the manager is wondering if the meal-delivery program is scraping the bottom of the volunteer barrel.

I knock loudly on Mary's door.

"Come in." There are tears in that voice.

I move into the room. Mary leans across the arm of her wheel chair, trying to punch numbers into her cordless phone. She slams down the phone.

"Dang it! That thing's not working! I'm sorry, did I swear? I'm sorry, honey."

I move to her. "It's okay. Can I help?"

Tears. "I can't get the right number."

The numbers on the touch pad of Mary's phone are enormous, but with her limited eyesight and the presence of

The Route

tears, it's obviously a problem.

"Could you dial this number?" She hands me a piece of paper on which she's scrawled six numbers.

"Sure." I look carefully at the numbers. "Is this a phone number, Mary?"

"Yes, it's my grandson's apartment."

"Jonathan's apartment?"

"Yes. He told me to call him back because he was having a fight with his dad." Tears come again. "Oh, Jonathan is so good to me. He's such a good boy."

"I know he is."

"His daddy is a bum. I hate to say it, but he is."

Mary's son Bill is an alcoholic—a marginal human when sober, and a very malicious person when drunk. Mary has shared horror stories of Bill's brutal treatment of his wife and Jonathan when Jonathan was growing up. Many times Mary would go to their house and cart her daughter-in-law and grandson out of harm's way. She stood up to Bill once, telling him that if he ever hurt his wife or Jonathan again, she'd put him in jail.

What a heartbreaking thing for a mother to have to do. Mothers certainly have their failings, but most cherish their children and hope they'll grow up to be part of the goodness of life. My heart aches for the battles Mary has fought over the years.

"Do you remember the number, Mary?"

"Not too good. That's why I wrote it down."

"Well, you only wrote down six numbers. You need seven."

"I only wrote six? Ohhh, I am so stupid." She puts her face

into her hands and sobs.

"No, you're not."

"It's his new apartment. It's a new number."

"I think you're just missing the last number. Let me read it to you, and see if you remember—5–5–5–6–1–8 . . ."

"Eight! There's another eight."

"See, that was easy." I pat her arm and write the second 8 on the paper.

"Would you dial that for me?" she asks, wiping her face on her sleeve.

"Of course." I think briefly about the other lunches, which are probably tepid by now. Not to worry. I turn to the task at hand, dialing the number and handing the phone to Mary. She sits anxiously through several rings.

"Hello? Is this Jonathan? Oh, sweetheart, are you all right?"

I leave her to her conversation and set out her meal. When I'm finished, I wave to her and move to leave. She waves back and mouths, "Thank you." I can see that she's calming down now that she knows Jonathan is okay. I shut the door behind me and take a deep breath. This job of being a parent never ends. As I become familiar with the friends on my route and learn their stories, I find amazing examples of caring and sacrifice as well as wounds and sorrow. Their experiences are helping me put things in my life into perspective. I didn't have to climb a mountain in Tibet for wisdom; I am informed every Thursday when I deliver a few cardboard containers of food. I also find it interesting how I'm becoming invested in their lives.

Bea is at the hairdressers again. Often her appointment falls

The Route

on a Thursday, so I just put her meal in the refrigerator with a smiley face on a sticky note. Like most of the other women on the route, Bea keeps her hair looking pretty spiffy. I've seen dynamite beauty-parlor colors, washes, and cuts by efficient aides, and even fancy perms given by daughters or daughters-in-law. The only person who cuts her own hair is Elaine, and that's a very scary proposition.

I knock on Elaine's door. No answer. I knock again. This is odd. Finally, there comes a hoarse voice from behind the door.

"Who is it?"

"It's Carol, Elaine." I know she's staring right at me through the peephole.

"Go away!"

"I have your lunch."

"Don't want it."

"What do you mean, you don't want it?" She doesn't answer. I knock softly. A small alarm is sounding in the back of my head. "Elaine, are you feeling okay?" I knock more loudly. "Elaine! Elaine, open the door!"

The door opens and Elaine stands staring at me like a mad cat. "Shut up! Quit making so much noise! They'll hear you." She *sounds* like a mad cat, too.

"Who?"

"The people who are trying to poison me. They put stuff in my food."

Man! This is weird. I haven't heard five words out of her mouth in the many months I've been delivering, and now this? I am totally at a loss as to how to handle the situation. Elaine starts to shove the door closed, so I stick a basket into

73

the opening. I hear the plastic crack. What if I'd stuck my foot in there?

"Elaine, no one has put anything into this food. I brought it from my vehicle to your door. It is good, nourishing food."

"I fed some to my grandson, and he died."

All right, we just zoomed past weird to bizarre. I stand staring at her with my mouth open, wanting to say something, but no sound comes out. I don't need to worry though, because Elaine is keeping up the conversation for both of us.

"I used to work seventy hours a week. Now all they want is my money. Watch out for that one lady in the office. She helps them take my mail. They go through my mail and get out my Social Security check."

"Elaine, I'm coming in to put your food in the refrigerator."

"I don't want it."

"Well, I have to leave it. It's in the rules." That's not actually true, but it rings with authority. I push against her door with my shoulder. Elaine backs out of the way.

"You can't make me eat poisoned food."

I take a quick visual scan of her apartment. It's hard to see much because all the window coverings are drawn.

"I'm going to turn on this kitchen light so I can see where to put stuff." The forty-watt glow anemically spills out of the kitchen and into the front room and hallway, showing a place sparsely furnished but clean. (I suppose I was expecting piles of newspapers and empty tuna-fish cans.) I turn to look at Elaine and have to keep myself from blurting out an expletive. Her skin is red and raw as though she's been scrubbing it with a wire brush. Her gray hair is cut at odd angles, and her clothing hangs on her as though she's lost a lot of weight. She keeps her distance and glares at me.

"Are your feet dirty?" she hisses.

"No. I washed them this morning."

"No, your shoes."

"My shoes are clean." I can't believe she's actually letting me stand inside her apartment.

She slaps my hand away from the basket. "You'd better not touch that food. The poison will go right through your skin."

I ignore her, picking up the containers and putting them on her counter. "Okay. Hunter's stew in a sealed container, tapioca pudding in a sealed container, green salad in a sort of sealed container, milk sealed, bread not sealed. I think the only thing you shouldn't eat is the bread."

She moves next to me in the kitchen, eyeing the food. "Not the bread?"

"No, not sealed. I wouldn't eat that, but everything else is sealed tight." I show her the strength of the seal. "Nothing is getting by that."

She touches the carton of tapioca pudding.

"This is safe?"

"Oh, yeah. Tough seal on that one."

"Maybe my grandson ate the bread, and it wasn't sealed."

"That's possible." I don't know why I'm playing along with her delusion, but it seems to be working.

She picks up the hunter's stew.

I look straight at her. "So, Elaine, here's what I think you should do—I think you should eat some of this good food."

Tears spill down her cheeks. "Maybe not. Not worth it."

Those five words speak a lifetime of disappointment, and I have no idea how to answer her without seeming trite. I put my hand on her arm. "I want to see you next Thursday."

She stands silently for the longest time, holding the hunter's stew and not rejecting my touch. "Okay."

"Okay."

She grips my sleeve. "Will you try and get that lady in the office to stop stealing my money?"

"I'll see what I can do." I pick up my baskets and move for the door. I know at the end of the route I'll be calling Valerie to tell her Elaine's situation, because someone from Adult Protective Services needs to come in and check on her. I also know that interfering may mean Elaine will be taken out of her apartment and placed in special care, but to not interfere means abandoning her to loneliness and delusion—or worse.

Through these fragile people, I've come to realize that perhaps the worst challenge they face at life's end is loneliness, their existence defined by the day-after-day drone of the television. I wonder how long it's been since Elaine has had a conversation with anyone, exchanging ideas and opinions? I'm sure my mind would falter if I were left alone for a long stretch of time with only my imagination to keep me company. I send out a wish in Elaine's behalf—for laughing friends and happy outings. I realize that I'm stretching the wish continuum extremely thin, but there's no harm in trying.

I shake myself into the here and now, and race off to Olea's apartment. Every week I figure I'll knock at an empty place, finding that Margaret has settled her in a nice assisted-living facility, where she can live her life well cared for, using up all of her selfish daughters' inheritance. Heaven.

I knock and Margaret answers the door.

"Hi, Carol."

"Hi, Margaret. How's she doing?"

"Same."

I look to find Olea in her usual spot, but she's not there.

"Where is she?"

"She's in her bedroom looking at a tree."

"A what?"

Margaret gives a derisive snort. "Tree. Here, come see." She leads me to the bedroom and opens the door a crack. It's dark inside.

"Oh! She's sleeping," I whisper, stepping back.

"No, she's not." Margaret calls out softly, "Olea, Carol's here. She wants to see your tree. Is it okay if she comes in?"

Olea's small voice returns from the darkness. "Of course."

We move into the dark room, and my eyes are drawn to a glimmering light source at the side of Olea's bed. On a corner table sits a small silver tree with hundreds of soft, swaying filaments for branches. At the end of each filament is a twinkle of colored light. Olea runs her crooked fingers through the light. "It's beautiful, isn't it?" she asks as we enter.

"It is," I answer, entranced by the magical illumination.

"My daughter sent it to me," she says proudly.

"Really? I . . . I mean, how nice," I stutter, hoping my voice sounds sincere.

Olea's voice trembles with emotion. "All the way from Arizona, for my birthday."

I perk up. "I didn't know it was your birthday?"

Olea hesitates, then asks, "Margaret, is it my birthday?"

"Last month, sweetie."

"Oh, last month," Olea answers softly. "Last month." She pulls her hand away from the tree. "Margaret, I'm going to take a little nap now."

"Okay, good idea."

"Can I leave my tree on?"

"Sure. Do you need some lunch?"

"No, I'm fine, thank you."

"I'll check on you in an hour."

We leave the room, and Margaret quietly shuts the door. She silently walks to the kitchen, and I follow. I don't speak, because Margaret looks like she wants to be kicking some skinny, bare legs with some steel-toed boots. She opens the door of the refrigerator and I hand her the food.

Margaret shakes her head and lets out a disgruntled sigh. "Her daughter wants her to come for a visit."

"Which daughter?"

"The Arizona daughter."

I'm confused. "Arizona? Could Olea make that trip?"

Margaret slams the refrigerator door. "No, of course not."

"I didn't think so. Doesn't her daughter realize that?"

"Of course she realizes it, but isn't she the kindest daughter for offering? Like Miss-Got-Money from Arizona couldn't just get her skinny butt on a plane and come here for a visit. She hasn't seen her mother in two years." Margaret is steamed. "And what's with the tree thing? She totally forgets her mom's birthday—not even a card, and then this gift shows up, UPS."

"Sounds like she wants something."

"Bingo! Isn't it interesting that the care facility just notified daughters number 1 and 2 that their mom will be taking up residence at the facility the end of the month? Now, daughter number 1 is calling, and daughter number 2 is sending trees."

"Sweet of them," I answer.

"Yeah, right. They want to sweetly strong-arm their mom into a less-expensive place so she won't use up so much of their inheritance. Piranha."

"Good description."

"This is one of the dearest, most uncomplaining women on the planet. She deserves caring and tenderness."

"She's had that from you, Margaret. She has."

Margaret stands looking at the floor. "Yeah, but that stuff should come from family."

In a perfect world, I think to myself.

Both of us are quiet. I'm trying to figure out how life could get so out of whack, and Margaret is probably doing the same. Finally I find my voice. "So, she goes into the home the end of this month?"

"Yep. Nice place. It'll be the best thing. They'll take excellent care of her 24/7."

I hear reluctant resolution in Margaret's voice. This angel in scrubs will have a hard time letting go, and to a lesser extent, so will I.

I sigh. "Well, I'd better get going. I have one lady on the route who chews off my ears if I'm late."

Margaret laughs. "Off you go, then. See you next time."

"Okay."

I head down the hall to Maxine's apartment. If I were a betting woman, I'd bet that Maxine wasn't home, and ten times out of ten, I'd be right. As I near her apartment, I notice the raspberry-colored sticky note. I love trying to guess where she's off to.

Dear lunch lady,

I am at the senior center playing pinochle with my friend Sadie. Please leave lunch with my neighbor.

Thanks, Maxine

I knock on her neighbor's door. After a few moments, the door opens.

"Yes?"

"Maxine said to . . ."

"Where to this time?"

"Pinochle."

"Gadabout. Hand it over."

I do.

"Anything else?"

"No."

"Okay, then." The door shuts with a snap.

I chuckle. Poor lady. She probably gets tired of stashing all of Maxine's lunches and not being invited to tag along on any of the adventures. Then again, she may enjoy being Keeper of the Lunch.

When I reach Ladora's door, I find she has a new sign: I'D RATHER BE SKIING. What a character. I hear raised voices from inside her apartment, and stand for a moment debating whether to interrupt or not. Actually there is no choice, as I have a lukewarm lunch here, getting cooler by the moment. I

The Route

knock, and the argument stops immediately. The door opens, and I'm presented with someone who walked off the pages of Vogue: pale yellow suit with silk blouse, pearl accessories, and pale yellow shoes. Man! I bet her nylons cost more than the only suit I own! Her shiny, dark brown hair is pulled tightly into a ponytail at the nape of her neck. Her eyes are a striking blue, and her skin and makeup are flawless. I stand there feeling drab, flat, and large.

Hey! I tell myself. *There are all sorts of people in the world. Some can be pretty, and some can be smart. I can't help it if I'm smart.* I laugh at my own joke.

"Hi, I'm Carol. You must be Kristine."

Kristine smiles a bright smile. "I am." I like her. Maybe we could become friends and she could give me pointers on how to color code my wardrobe, or what's the hottest new thing in makeup.

Ladora calls out to me. "Hi, Carol! Come on in!" She sounds glad to have me as a distraction. Kristine steps back and lets me past. She smells lightly of Chanel No. 5.

The fashion model/architect follows me into the room to retrieve her handbag. "Mom, I'm going to take off. I have a one o'clock meeting."

"Okay, honey."

"We'll talk more about this."

"Okay."

Kristine comes over and gives her mom a hug. Such a contrast—the pale yellow three-hundred-dollar suit, and the twenty-dollar Grand Canyon t-shirt.

"And no more sweets for a while," Kristine instructs.

Ladora was right. Her daughter is bossy, but I can tell she really loves her mother. Kristine turns to smile at me as I'm unloading Ladora's lunch onto the counter.

"You know, they could make those meals much more savory without adding any salt."

"Really?" *Who does she think I am, one of the main chefs at meal preparation?*

"Just some imaginative use of different herbs and spices."

"Hmm. Interesting," I say, trying to look as if I know what the heck she's talking about. *Maybe she thinks I'm Paula Deen and have some pull at the Food Network.* "If I were you," I say sincerely, "I'd call the food place and give them your suggestions."

"Really?"

Of course. Your mom says you're a great cook, and I'm sure they could use some new recipes. Just call the main number, and have them put you in touch with the food . . . people."

She smiles. "Okay, maybe I will. Thanks." She picks up her carry bag. "'Bye, Mom. See you Saturday."

"'Bye, honey."

Kristine exits elegantly, and it takes a minute for her presence in the room to dissipate.

"Wow! Your daughter is beautiful, Ladora."

"Yep. Pretty snazzy. That's all her father—Mr. Charm and Handsome. I just carried her around for nine months. Now, her older brothers take after me. Plain as mud hens."

"Ladora!"

"The truth is the truth. Doesn't hurt to tell it. So, what's for lunch?"

The Route

"Hunter's stew."

"Yum. Now, Kristine would probably say this is dull and bland. Bossy, isn't she?"

"A little."

"More than a little. She's trying to make me go on some trip with their family, and I don't want to go."

"Why not? Don't you want to travel?"

"I do, but, I'd have to get on an airplane, and I'm not getting on any airplane."

"You've never been on an airplane?"

"No!" Her exaggerated look of fear makes me laugh.

"They really are safe," I say with confidence.

Ladora glowers at me. "Now, don't you be siding with her."

I chuckle and continue to set out her food. "Where are they going?"

"New England states in September."

"Oh, Ladora! You would love that! Little New England towns, the beautiful fall colors."

"Cut it out. Don't you have other meals to deliver? They're probably stone cold by now." She's pushing me out the door, and I'm laughing.

"Okay, okay. I can take a hint. But I think you should think about it."

"Traitor."

The door shuts on my backside. I shake my head and smile. What a day! I've gone through so many emotions that I'm completely worn out. And it's not over yet. I have three more stops, with Sidewinder Viola waiting at the end of the trail.

I forgot to drop off pudding at Maxine's, and I'm hoping to

use that as my trump card. Extra food usually gives me some grace time with Viola, and I'm hoping tapioca's good for at least ten minutes.

I find Lucille and Betty in front of their house when I pull up. Lucille is pushing Betty in a wheelchair towards a tan and rust Volkswagen van. There's an elderly man standing beside the van, shifting his weight from one leg to the other. When I pull up, he turns and heads for the back of the house. Lucille yells something at him—harsh words I fortunately can't make out.

As I get out of the SUV, I can see that Betty is tied into the wheelchair with an old tea towel; it's the only thing keeping her from falling out, as she obviously has no ability to hold herself upright.

Lucille turns from the wheelchair and yells. "Marv, you toad! Get your butt out here! I'm gonna kick it from here to Cleveland." She turns to me. "Could you go see what that fool's doing?"

I jump. "Me? Sure."

"Just have Marv put the food in the fridge."

"Okay." I move around the side of the house in pursuit of Mystery Marv. Who is this guy? In the many months I've been delivering meals to Lucille and Betty, I've never seen him.

The back screen door closes with a bang. I think Marv is avoiding me. I arrive at the back door and knock. No answer. I can see through the screen mesh into the kitchen and then into the hallway and the corner of a bedroom. Or maybe it's a storage room. There's no sign of Marv. I knock again.

"Hello? Marv? Lucille wanted you to put this food in the refrigerator, then come and help her."

The Route

No response.

"Marv? Hello?"

A timid voice comes from a back room. "Did she say she'd kick my butt?"

"She did."

"Just a minute, okay?"

"Okay." I look down at my feet so I won't be snooping in the kitchen. Off to the side of the back porch is a beat-up cardboard box filled with empty beer cans. Whoa! Either they've been saving up a while for recycling, or somebody in the house is awfully thirsty, or they need the AA phone number. I look back at my feet to stop my spying and prejudging. Who knows the pain that sits cooped up within those rooms?

Marv comes shuffling into the kitchen. He's a dreadfully thin man with stooped shoulders and messy gray hair. He opens the screen door and reaches for the basket. His cheeks and chin are covered in stubble.

I force myself not to stare. "Oh, here's your paper."

His head nods several times as he takes it. He sets the paper on the table and unloads the basket without once looking up or giving any indication that he wants conversation. I respect his solitude. He comes back to the door and hands me the basket.

"Thanks, ma'am."

"You're welcome." I turn away without further comment. As I round the side of the house I see that Lucille has Betty at the van and is untying the tea towel.

I move towards them. "Do you need any help?"

"No, thanks. We're just taking her to the doctors. Is Marv coming?"

"I think so."

Lucille growls. "Stupid idiot."

I cringe. I remember once calling my sister that name within hearing range of my mom. I was sent to my room and had to miss *Zorro*. I've never called a person that since.

Marv comes sheepishly around the side of the house. I don't think he wants a trip to Cleveland.

Lucille yells at him. "Get over here and help me! What were you thinking, running off like that?"

I move quietly to my vehicle, throwing the basket into the back and hopping in. As I wait to pull out onto the busy street, I watch Lucille and Marv gently lifting Betty into the van. They have a hard time holding on to her because of the involuntary jerking of her arms and legs. Betty was afflicted with this debilitating disease at nineteen—she's now thirty-five. My heart lurches. Lucille and Marv have given fifteen years of soul-numbing sacrifice to their daughter, yet if we saw them on the street, separated from their circumstance, we'd probably see them as steerage. We'd shake our heads, wondering how people could so mangle life's precious opportunities, or we might say, "There but for the grace of God, go I."

Marv struggles to put Betty's wheelchair into the van. His arms look like twigs. He finally secures it and gives Lucille the thumbs up. She pats him on the back and heads for the driver's side of the van.

A car honks and a young man in a green Jeep motions me onto the road. I wave and pull out. My mind is in such a muddle that I forget where I'm going and turn the wrong direction at the cross street, going four blocks before realizing my mistake.

Joyce is never concerned if I'm late, but I don't think an extra pudding is going to get me a pardon from Viola today.

Lilacs are blooming around Joyce's yard, and her white metal lawn chairs sit invitingly on the side patio. I hope she's been able to get outside and enjoy the spring sunshine. When she was younger, one of her favorite activities was gardening.

I knock on her door and go in. Her gravelly voice comes from the back of the house. "Hello, Carol. I'm in the kitchen." What a mind she has, remembering my name and the day I deliver from that very first Thursday.

As I move through the front room I can smell fresh cigarette smoke. Impossible. I step into the kitchen to find Joyce sitting in her usual place involved in her usual activity—smoking. I'm so angry I feel like slamming my basket on the counter. Joyce reads my face.

"Are you all right?" she wheezes.

"I—I—" Checking my emotion, I stop my mouth too. I have to remember that she's addicted and is not likely to give up her habit now at the end of her life, even after two surgeries and a painful lung disease. I don't understand how the big tobacco companies can be so brutally inhuman.

"What's wrong, honey?"

"I'm fine, Joyce. I'm just worried about you."

She looks down at her hands, and I watch her laboring to breathe. I quietly place her lunch out on the counter. After a time, her words come with great effort.

"Did you finish that article you were writing? Wasn't it for young people?"

I'm stunned. "How did you remember that?"

A smile touches the corner of her mouth. "High IQ."

"I would say so," I answer. I cringe as she throws her cigarette butt into her unfinished orange juice, but I force myself to keep talking. "Yep. I finished it about a week ago."

"Good for you. And what was the topic?"

I hesitate. "It was an article about making choices. I sent it off to the magazine a couple of days ago, so keep your fingers crossed."

"Will do." She concentrates on her breathing, each short intake so painful that she winces.

I feel sick to my stomach. "Is Alex coming today?"

She nods.

"Good. Okay, then. I'll be off and let you have him all to yourself."

She smiles weakly.

I go to her and put my hand on her hand. Her skin is transparent. "I'll see you next Thursday."

She nods and I turn to leave. I move into her quiet front room where tokens and memorabilia from her past cover side tables, curio cabinets, and wall space. I pass by the picture of Joyce in her military uniform. She was a medical nurse during World War II, serving in the Philippines, and was nearly captured by the Japanese. Her picture shows a woman not easy to decipher. Hiding behind a mask of determination is a soul of brashness and mischief. After getting to know Joyce, it doesn't surprise me that she evaded enemy capture and saved several other nurses at the same time.

I'm so busy contemplating the puzzle of life that I'm surprised when I find myself pulling up in front of Viola's

Airstream. I discover the little fashion queen madly clipping the rose bushes that front her chain-link fence. She seems unaware of the time, being so caught up in her horticulture. Her bright green duster and yellow tie belt is vogue flower-trimming attire, to which she's added a stylish yet practical fishing hat, and floral garden gloves. For footwear, she's gone with the ever-smart pink tennis shoe.

As I pull the vehicle into her driveway, she looks up and smiles. Smiles? Is there something weird in the spring air, or has she been using bug spray?

"Good morning!" she chirps brightly.

Boy! She *has* lost track of time.

"Good morning, Viola," I call. "Look at your gorgeous rose bushes."

"Well, they'll be even better when I'm done with them." She snips off several more stems as I approach warily with her lunch.

"You sure have been working hard."

"Most of the morning, and I'm half starved to death."

"It's hunter's stew today."

"Oh, one of my favorites."

"And an extra pudding."

"Goodie! Just stick it up there on my milk box, and I'll be right along."

Goodie? I've never seen her so cheerful. Did she find religion or something? I step onto the stoop and begin unpacking her lunch. A flutter of white catches the corner of my eye, and I look up. There, on the yard side of her chain-link fence, hangs a tattered bra and several pairs of panties. *Well, laundry too!* She

89

has had a busy morning.

Viola walks into the yard, wiping her forehead with the back of her gloved hand. "Double frog spit, I'm tired. I'm gonna eat that lunch and go straight to bed. What time is it?"

"I'm not sure. My watch is busted." Liar. I am not going to the good place.

Viola takes off her gloves, walks over, and checks her laundry. "Can't beat that. Who needs a dumb dryer when you've got the wind and the sun?" She removes her bra and panties from the fence, and heads for the stoop. I figure I'd better get while the gettin's good.

"Okay then, Viola. I'll see you next Thursday."

"Okay. And it would be nice if you could be on time."

Crunch. I am a bug under her shoe.

I keep moving. "Okay. Enjoy your extra pudding." Did I put a little too much emphasis on the word *extra?*

"Okay." She picks up the hunter's stew and moves into her trailer. I turn and make some sort of childish face.

"Well, okay then. Okey dokey. Okey smokey." I mumble myself back to the car, but I find I can't keep up the pretense of being miffed, because the vision of Viola's panties keeps fluttering into my imagination. I start laughing. What a day! I climb into the SUV, exhausted and woozy from the emotional rollercoaster, and head for the senior center. As soon as I drop off all the stuff, I'm heading home and—double frog spit—*I'm* taking a nap!

CHAPTER 5

Byways

The best stories are the ones that are true, and I found that the lives of my Thursday friends began to expand beyond their small living spaces as I was trusted with the stories of their pasts: Goldie growing up in a trailer park in Arizona and falling in love with the manager's son at the Motel 6 where she worked as a maid; Bea, whose father, an investment consultant in Chicago, forbid her to marry Randolf because he was a poor struggling student—the same Randolf who would go on to own his own medical research company and make sufficient money to make Bea's father eat crow; Joyce marrying a private in the army only to lose him six weeks later in the battle of Midway. Their reminiscences were engaging and amazing, and I found myself starting the route earlier every week so I would not be robbed of story time.

The Last Emperor Tom had a story that merited a full-length documentary on the History Channel. I would sit at his small kitchen table with my chin in my hand, mesmerized by his soft dialect.

"I was born Mei Ping Hsu in Yanjing, China, in 1915. My father was merchant who brought goods to our town from Chongqing. I had older brother and two younger sisters. We always laughed at our mother. She was very funny woman—

daughter of old world—very superstitious."

I laugh as he imitates his mother.

"'Mei Ping, cover your head when you walk under full moon, or demons will enter your brain, and you'll be man without sense. Eyi! Mei Ping! Do not cut your toenails at night! That will bring visit from ghost . . . or your dead grandmother. You don't want her visiting. She was very unlucky woman!'"

He talks about growing to manhood in the China of Sun Yatsen and Chiang Kai-Shek. I've seen pictures of these men in history books, but now they're real to me.

"Then Communists came, and Mao Tsetung." Tom shakes his head and changes the subject. "Thirteenth day of May 1935 was happy day for me. I marry When Shan. My mother was happy woman, because she was one who made match."

He talks about joining the military of Chiang Kai-Shek, becoming a colonel at a very young age, and standing against the Communists. He talks about fighting in vicious battles against the Japanese when they invaded China. I look at his slender build and gentle laugh and cannot imagine him as a soldier.

"Times were bad when Mao Tsetung and Communists take power, so When Shan and I decide to take children and go to island of Taiwan. My mother would not come with us. She said, 'Mei Ping, do not worry about me. You must go and build new life. Take family and find peace.'" He looks out the window. "She was poor, but she gave us cooked rice to eat on train." Tom is silent for some time. He looks at me and shakes his head. "I never saw her again."

I can empathize with his loss, knowing exactly what that feels like. This time, *I* change the subject. "So how did you

The Route

decide to come to America?"

He smiles. "We have many children, so I tell When Shan I want to move to bigger house. She says, 'Much bigger house?' and I say, 'Yes, much bigger house, far away.'" He taps his finger on his forehead. "She says, 'Where, Kaohsiung, Taipei?'" He's laughing now. "I say, 'No . . . I want to move where my cousin lives, and she says, 'Hong Kong?'" He claps his hands. "I say, 'No . . . I want to live by my other cousin in Boston, America!'"

I laugh with him. "What did When Shan say to that?"

He laughs, wiping tears from his eyes. "She says, 'Where can I find crates?'" He smiles at his wife's photograph. "So, I take on American name of Tom, and she is May, and we take our children and leave China." He pats my hand. "We were never sorry one day."

Amazing stories. Amazing people. I smile at Tom and count my blessings. If I hadn't seen the advertisement in the supermarket that day, or taken a chance at volunteering, I would have missed out on being a small part of their astonishing lives.

CHAPTER 6

U Turns

Summer was hotter than brimstone. Most of the seniors were thrilled because for once, without having their heaters up to eighty-five degrees, their fingers and toes were warm. The rest of us youngsters sullenly endured nature's blast furnace, wishing for trips to Vermont or Alaska.

Goldie's daughter-in-law, Janet, would sit with her out back under the cherry tree with iced lemonade and Fig Newtons, until the mid-morning sizzle forced them indoors to the swamp cooler. I would come around back, through the side gate, and find them clipping coupons, doing needlepoint, or working on Goldie's stamp collection.

"Morning, Goldie!" I exclaimed one day.

"Good-morning, my dear. What's for lunch?"

"Turkey sandwich, side lettuce and tomatoes, cold peaches. Hi, Janet."

"Morning, Carol. Here, let me put that stuff in the refrigerator. Goldie, you're not hungry right now, are you?"

"Oh, no. I ate too many cookies this morning. Janet, would you please turn down the swamp cooler while you're in there?"

"She hates the fake air," Janet says, smiling.

"I just hate that fake air," Goldie echoes.

"See, told ya." Another smile.

It was the only time I'd ever heard Goldie complain about anything, and I found it comforting. You see, I'd been comparing my lopsided life with her life of order and grace, and I'd found myself coming up short—way short. I'd forgotten a generational family rule that states: *Don't compare yourself to others because you'll always come out better or behind. Better will make you feel superior and entrap you in pride—behind will make you feel inferior and entrap you in doubt.* Big philosophy.

I vow to keep things in perspective. After all, I remind myself, Goldie's life of seeming perfection was arrived at over time—molded by years of decisions and experiences, tempered by tragedy, and softened by joy. She took the tools given to her at birth, and she engineered her existence. Now it's true, some people seem to start out with better tools, while others struggle with overwhelming obstacles. Nonetheless, we all have to maneuver the route as best we can, acquiring better tools along the way if we started out with junk, throwing broken tools in the garbage, and sharing our Craftsman tools if we have been so blessed. That is the point after all, isn't it—to get to the end of the road with something we've built in one hand and a friend at our side?

"Goldie."

"Yes, my dear."

"May I ask you a personal question?"

Her eyes sparkle. "Oh, those are the best kind."

"Is Robert your only child?"

"Only one living. I lost one at birth—a daughter—and a boy in a car accident. He was just out of high school."

I feel tears at the back of my throat. "I'm so sorry."

"It's all right. Life is like that sometimes."

I nod.

"I thought I was going to lose Robert a few years back." She leans forward to whisper me into her confidence. "Too much drinking."

I nod again. "I know the feeling."

She pats my hand. "You have a drinker?"

"Drugs, actually. Our son." I can't believe I'm sharing this with her. I've never shared this truth with anyone outside the immediate family, but Goldie's face is full of understanding and compassion.

"Is he getting help? Going to AA or anything?"

I shake my head. "I've started going to Al-Anon."

Goldie squeezes my hand. "Good girl. That'll help. It helped me."

"You went to Al-Anon?"

"I did." A tear slides down my cheek and suddenly Goldie's charity surrounds me like a blanket. "Oh, you sweet thing, don't give up," she says kindly.

"I could never do that." My voice is strained with a sadness I'm trying hard to control. "We had to ask him to leave the house."

"Well, they do have to know there are limits."

I stare into Goldie's sweet face and realize she's telling me the truth. I take a deep breath and feel a modicum of pain melting away.

"Just keep loving him, and remember that God has no grandchildren."

I ponder this comforting thought. How kind of Goldie to

share my sorrow and help me see things through wiser eyes.

Janet returns. "Your lunch is in the fridge, Miss Goldie, and I put in a load of laundry."

"Thank you, my dear." Goldie turns her attention back to me and squeezes my hand.

I stand and busy myself with gathering the lunch basket. "I'd better be going."

"I will see you next time, Miss Carol. Enjoy this beautiful day."

I smile at her, a new bond between us. "I will. Thank you."

Janet walks me to the side gate.

"She is the dearest person."

Janet nods. "She is."

I steady my emotions. "We talked a little about her life. You'd never know she's been through so much."

"True enough. She is mostly sunshine."

"She does look tired, though."

Janet brushes hair away from her face. "She had a tough weekend. We think she might have had a little stroke."

"Really?"

"Yeah. Her doctor told us this would start happening." There are tears in Janet's eyes.

Janet is a very private person, and I know she doesn't want a cry fest so I opt for a fast exit. "Well, I'd better get a move on. See you next Thursday."

"Okay, Carol. Thanks." Janet turns back to Goldie as I move off to the SUV.

I wish I could see Goldie waving to me from the window—

one more signal of encouragement. I try not to think of the implication of a possible stroke for sweet little Goldie. I take a deep breath, reminding myself that death is part of the process. Off we go to some other cosmos, or Karma, or heaven, trailing clouds of glory. I'm just hoping that if we make it to the good place, we'll get to be totally magnificent. I want smaller pores and the ability to do math. We'll also get to hang out with all the cool people like Mother Teresa and Abraham Lincoln and Goldie. Every Saturday night I'll go to my Nana's heavenly abode and have pot roast. Of course, it'll taste like pot roast, but it won't actually be pot roast because I doubt we'll be eating our animal friends. And speaking of animal friends, I'll have all my dogs back, and I'll have my dad back, and me and my dad and my dogs will take long walks together, and my dad won't have diabetes or cancer anymore. And we'll have forever to talk about relationships and tell each other funny jokes and figure out how to balance my checkbook. Heaven.

I arrive at the apartment building still pondering existence and pot roast. As I step out of my air-conditioned vehicle, the afternoon heat presses against me like I'm wearing a wool sweater in the Sahara. Yikes! It has to be a hundred degrees. I load the baskets quickly and head for the sanctuary of the building's dim, cool hallway. Ha! The joke's on me. As I step through the glass entry door, the temperature differential from outside to inside is maybe two degrees. I expect to find all my seniors slumped over their crossword puzzles with heat exhaustion.

I knock on Tom's door.

"Ah, come in! Come in!"

The Route

"Morning, Tom."

"Is Thursday Girl!"

I smile and move gratefully into the apartment. Talk about heaven! The temperature is probably eighty-two degrees, but after outside and the hallway, it feels like Minnesota in April.

"Ahh. It feels great in here." I set the baskets on the counter.

"Is so hot outside?"

"It's very hot."

"You okay, carry heavy basket?"

"Oh, sure. I'm strong." I flex the bicep on my carrying arm. Tom laughs. "Oh, very strong!"

I glance over to the picture of Tom's family. He and May sit center front as their seven children horseshoe around them. The older children look sedate like their parents, while the youngest two show a very American bravado.

"Sandwich today?"

"Yep. Turkey."

"Oh, turkey is good."

"There's also peaches."

"I like peaches."

"You like any fruit, Mr. Tom."

"I do."

I shake my head and grin. "Ninety-three and still eating apples."

He chuckles. "Yes, I like apple."

"Amazing."

"I have strong teeth." He smiles to show off his teeth. "Oh! Guess what?"

99

"What?"

"No. You guess."

"Umm . . . you're learning to golf."

He laughs. "No golf."

"You're getting a job."

He covers his face and laughs harder. "No. No job."

"You robbed a bank."

"I no rob bank! I no rob bank!" He holds on to the edge of the counter as his body shakes with laughter.

I'm pulled into the net of his gaiety, and soon the two of us are jiggling about like caught tunas. Oh, my sides ache, and I figure this can't possibly be good for someone who's ninety-three. Finally, with gasps and gulps and hiccups, we calm down.

"You are very bad woman."

"Me? You started it."

His eyes twinkle mischievously as he wipes away the laughter tears. I still have a hard time picturing him in a military uniform fighting Communists.

"So, guess what."

"Tom!" We both start to chuckle again. "Now, cut that out! My sides hurt. No more guessing."

"Okay, okay, I tell you. I'm going on trip."

"Really?"

"Only little trip. Phyllis is driving me to Winford to visit son."

"Your oldest?"

"No, youngest, Michael. He open restaurant."

"Italian?"

Tom opens his mouth to reply, then starts laughing again.

The Route

"Oh, you very bad woman."

"Sorry. So, when are you going?"

"Tomorrow. Come back Sunday."

I pick up my baskets. "Well, have a great time."

"Yes, great time. Here, I get door."

"Thank you. See you next Thursday."

"Next Thursday, Thursday Girl."

I look at him sternly. "And no more laughing today."

He chuckles. "Okay, no laughing."

I find it hard to keep my own directive as I giggle my way down the hall. I make a vow that if life begins to look dreary, I'll watch a Little Rascal's movie, play miniature golf, ride a bike, or have the neighbor kids over for Kick the Can. Of course, I can always call my friends, and we'll go to lunch and laugh our heads off about the crazy things that have gone on in our lives. Life. Bring it on.

I knock on Mary's door. No answer. I knock again and notice that her I'M OKAY sign isn't out. I put my ear against the door but don't hear any movement. In the months I've been delivering her meals, this is the first time she hasn't answered. I knock again—loudly. Nothing. I try the door. Locked. I'm starting to panic as one of the apartment managers comes down the hallway.

"Excuse me, do you know where Mary is? She's on my list for lunch today, but she doesn't answer, and her sign isn't out."

"Mary?" She checks the papers on her clipboard. "Just says 'out for the day.'"

"Oh. So, she's not in there?"

"No. Out for the day."

"So, maybe somebody came to take her out for the day, out to lunch or something."

The manager raises her eyebrows. "Could be."

"Okay. So, they probably just didn't get her name off my list."

The manager is moving away. "That would be my guess."

"Well, thank you."

"You're welcome." She escapes around the corner.

Out for the day. Well, that's good. Mary doesn't get many opportunities to be out for the day.

I take off for Bea's, who isn't home either. She's at the hairdressers, so I do the usual smiley-face note on her meal and stick it in the refrigerator.

I stop in front of Elaine's apartment and think good thoughts for her. It's become sort of a mini-ritual with me. After I called Valerie that spring day, she alerted people from Adult Protective Services to check on Elaine. They determined she couldn't live on her own anymore and placed her in a secured care facility. The next Thursday, when I saw that her name had been squeezed off my list, I felt guilty yet relieved. I still haven't sorted out my feelings, so I stop at her door and wish her well.

I move on to Olea's apartment. Just as I'm about to knock, the door flies open and two large men emerge—one carrying an empty bookcase and the other a bed mattress.

The mattress man nearly whacks me. "Oh, sorry."

"No problem. Is Olea in?"

"Who?"

"The woman who lives here."

The Route

"Oh, yeah. She's in the front room with her nurse."

I make my way inside.

"Hi, Margaret."

"Hi, Carol!"

"Is she finally off to Regency Park?"

"She is." Margaret leans down to Olea. "It's moving day, isn't it, sweetie?"

Olea points at the door where the moving men just exited. "Margaret, are you sure they're being careful?"

"Yes. I'm keeping a close eye on them."

Olea sits in her special wheelchair staring at the boxes in concern. I kneel down next to her. "Hi, Olea."

She takes my hand. "I'm going to my new place today."

"I know. Margaret told me."

Margaret nods. "Yep. No more roadblocks. Those girls slowed things down for a while, but no more, isn't that right, Olea?"

"No more roadblocks."

"She is off to the Buckingham Palace of care facilities."

Olea smiles and I sense her excitement.

"I'm so glad it worked out," I tell her.

"It's a lovely place," she says in a whisper. "Margaret found it for me, and it's lovely."

"And she told me that someone will be there for you all the time."

Olea's head bobs several times. "I'll like that. Sometimes I get nervous when I'm by myself."

"Of course." I pat her hand. "Should I leave your lunch?"

"I am hungry today. Will there be time, Margaret?"

"Plenty. These guys are not the fastest movers in the country."

Olea grins. "Snails."

"Right, snails," Margaret concurs.

I'm amazed that they're both in such good moods. I thought this day would be difficult for them, but it seems I'm the only one having separation anxiety. I move to the kitchen to set out Olea's lunch, and Margaret follows.

"You okay?" Margaret asks.

"I guess so. I just can't believe how attached I am to these cute people. Five, ten minutes once a week, and I'm hooked."

Margaret nods. "Yeah."

"I can't even imagine what *you're* feeling."

"Actually, I'm feeling great! Olea is going to a fantastic facility, and hopefully she'll live there so long her dumb daughters won't get a dime."

I laugh and realize I'm going to miss angel Margaret's tell-it-like-it-is approach to life. I take the wrapping off the lunch, make sure everything's cut into small pieces, put the straw into the milk carton, and find Olea's special spoon. Margaret helps me carry the meal to Olea's chair, where we arrange everything just so. Olea tries to look up at me, so I kneel down by her side.

"I probably won't see you again," she starts. Tears jump into my eyes. "Thank you for bringing my lunch and talking to me." I can only manage a nod. "Would you please say thank you to all the other lunch people?"

"Sure." I look up and see Margaret crying. *Great, I'll never get control of myself now.* I take Olea's crooked hand. "I'm glad

The Route

you're moving to Buckingham Palace," I whisper.

Olea grins. "Me too." She wipes a tear off my cheek. "Margaret, would you please get the lunch lady a tissue before she waters my sandwich?"

I laugh through my tears. "Sorry."

She pats my hand. "Be good."

"Okay." I linger for a moment more, helping Olea get her fingers around the handle of her special spoon.

"Thank you."

"You're welcome." I stand and head for the kitchen.

Margaret gives me a tissue and a hug. "Thanks for all you've done, Carol."

"A few minutes, once a week?" I shake my head. "You're the one, Margaret. You're amazing." I pick up my baskets. Margaret hands me another tissue and opens the door. I nearly bump into the movers, who have finally come back for another load. I sidestep out of their way.

"Sorry," I say.

"No problem." They push past me into the room. "So, what's next?"

The door closes and I move off down the hallway. I stop for a moment in the apartment lobby to blow my nose and admire the patriotic decorations. Pictures of early famous Presidents, and red, white, and blue bunting festoon the walls, and a small replica of the Statue of Liberty sits on the center coffee table, surrounded by artificial red, white, and blue carnations.

The manager with the clipboard comes into the lobby, not noticing me at first, intent on her papers. She glances up just as I'm stuffing the used tissue into my pocket and picking up my baskets. I smile but can tell by the look on her face that she remembers our earlier encounter. She looks back to her clipboard and heads directly for the office.

I head for Maxine's, wondering where she's gallivanting today. When I get to her apartment, there's no note. *That's odd.* I knock.

"Just a minute!"

She's home? That's very odd.

"I'll be right there!"

I stand anxiously, like a kindergartener waiting to recite in the class assembly. I don't even remember what Maxine looks like. The door opens, and I'm face to face with Barbara Bush.

"May I help you?"

"I—I'm—I have your lunch."

"Great! Come on in."

I walk in and get another shock. Maxine's neighbor from across the hall is sitting at the table working on a puzzle of Dalmatian puppies, or maybe it's dominoes. Her arm shoots into the air. "Got another edge piece."

Maxine grins at her friend's enthusiasm. "Great!" She turns her First-Lady face to me. "I don't think we've met."

Her neighbor snorts. "She's only been around for months, Maxine, if you'd ever stay home."

"Really? Sorry."

"That's okay. Your neighbor . . ."

"Beth."

"Beth's always good about taking your meal."

"Like I have a choice?" Beth snorts.

Maxine chuckles. "Oh, find some more edge pieces." She

extends her hand to me. "I'm Maxine, and this is my friend Beth."

"Hi. I'm Carol. Has anyone ever told you that you look like . . ."

"Yes, many times. You know, Carol, I do remember you. Didn't you come that one time with Valerie?"

"That was my first day."

"You looked stunned."

"Stunned? Yes, that's about right. I don't remember much about that first day."

"Found another edge piece!"

"Good work, Miss Beth!"

"Where would you like your lunch, Maxine?"

"On the counter, please."

"Actually, I have an extra if you'd like me to leave it. One of my ladies was out for the day."

"Really?" Maxine turns toward her friend. "Beth would you like to join me for lunch?"

"How much will it cost me?"

Maxine smiles. "Six dollars and fifty cents."

"Highway robbery."

"We'd love the extra lunch. Thank you." She looks out to her small back patio. "I wonder if it's too hot for a picnic."

I vow to be Maxine when I'm old—easygoing, gracious, active, and interesting. Yep, basic Maxine with a little of Mary, Ladora, and Goldie sprinkled in for good measure. Oh, and of course I couldn't leave out Bea's sweetness, or Viola's fashion sense.

"Allergies?" Maxine questions.

"I beg your pardon?"

"I just wondered if you have allergies. Your eyes are all red and puffy."

I hadn't even considered what my face must look like after my cry fest at Olea's.

Maxine pats my arm. "Shame on me. That's a very personal question, and none of my business."

"It's okay. It's not allergies. I had to say good-bye to someone."

"I understand. You had a good cry."

I'm feeling a bit awkward, like I did when I had to tell my high school guidance counselor why I was found crying in the sports equipment closet. Then it hits me what Maxine just said. She called it a *good* cry. I smile. "Yes, that's exactly what I had. A good cry."

"I just love a good cry!" Maxine chimes. "How about you, Beth?"

"Nope. Never do it."

Maxine is incredulous. "How do you manage that?"

"I just don't get emotional."

"That's pretty weird, Beth. What do you do when they play the national anthem?"

"Sing."

Maxine and I burst out laughing.

Beth is not amused. "Are you gonna help me with this puzzle or not?"

"Of course, you crazy old loon." Maxine shakes her head. "You sing. I mean it, Beth, you take the cake."

I pick up my baskets. "You two have a nice lunch, and I'll

see you next Thursday."

Beth snorts. "Or, maybe not, if Ms. Gadabout is out roaming the countryside."

"And next time, you're coming with me," Maxine states.

Beth snorts again. "I'm too old for adventures."

"Piffle," Maxine says dismissively. "We're just old enough to understand the marvel of adventures. Red Hat Ladies, here we come!"

Beth shakes her head. "And she calls me a crazy old loon."

Maxine walks me to the door, calling back over her shoulder. "See if I invite you to lunch again."

"Cold day in hell, I'd say."

Maxine chuckles. "Isn't she the limit?"

"Quite a character."

"I can hear you."

"And ears like a fox. Thanks for the lunches, Carol."

"You're welcome."

"Hey! Are you gonna help, or not?" Beth's tone indicates mock annoyance.

Maxine shakes her head. "Well, I guess I'm needed. See you next time." She smiles and closes the door.

What a pair.

Only Ladora's lunch is left in my basket, and I head off to the land of dime-store wonders with a light step. Over several months, Ladora has added a ceramic burro, an ugly Norwegian troll, and two more Chia pets to her collection. As much as her architect daughter complains about Ladora's eccentric sense of decorating, I think the items are woven into her heart, and I see a time, after Ladora's passing, when a ceramic burro and an ever-blooming cactus sit next to someone's Steinway piano and Duncan Fife chairs.

I knock on Ladora's door and wait. I hear music from inside the apartment—some sort of peppy Calypso. I knock a little louder.

"Oh, hang on a second!"

I hang on for twelve seconds and the door pops open.

"Hello! Come on in!" She's winded, and she's wearing a powder blue jogging outfit.

Her flushed face takes me by surprise. "Have you been jogging?"

She fans herself. "No. Mercy! Me, jogging?"

"Dancing?"

"No." She smiles and catches her breath. "Chair exercising with Marcus."

I'm not sure I want details. I enter the room cautiously, expecting an old guy in a lion tamer's outfit to suddenly jump out of the closet.

"I just found him. The local cable channel."

Ah! Marcus is a sixty-five-year-old TV exercise hunk with gorgeous gray hair and a body like Steven Segal.

"Handsome, ain't he?"

"Very."

Marcus stands behind his TV chair doing neat little leg squats. Ladora is mesmerized.

"My Jimmy was handsome too." She goes to her bookshelf, brings back a small photo album, and hands it to me. "Here, I'll let you see for yourself."

Flipping open the album, I find an exquisitely good-looking

young man in a military uniform. I love black and white photos because they show so much detail. Jimmy's dark wavy hair is combed back, accentuating classic Adonis features: perfect nose, high cheekbones, soft lips. Yummy.

"Okay, okay, quit drooling."

"Wow! He was amazing, Ladora."

"Told ya. That's why Kristine looks like she does. His family all look like that. They couldn't understand why their darling boy married somebody plain like me."

"Ladora."

"Hey, plain's fine. Jimmy loved me like I was a movie star. My mom loved Jimmy because he had substance. He wasn't even bugged when his first two boys came out looking like me."

"You're a character."

"And proud of it."

I hand Ladora the album, and she flips through the pages while I set out her lunch. She is years away, reliving experiences and emotions—washing the black and whites with all the color of her memories.

"He's been gone ten years." She turns another page. "Buster and Jimmy Jr. could make their daddy laugh till he nearly busted a gut. Good thing, too, cause Jimmy could get a little serious. That's where Kristine gets it."

"And being bossy?" I ask carefully.

"Oh, no. She picked that one up on her own."

Ladora returns the album to the bookshelf and turns off the TV.

"Keep exercising if you want to. Don't let me stop you."

"No thanks. I've had enough for today."

"Not your idea of a good time?"

She grunts. "Kristine told me I had to get in shape if I'm going on the trip."

"You're going?"

"Probably."

"Ladora, that's terrific!"

"Well, I don't know about terrific. They're gonna have to knock me out to get me on that airplane."

"You'll be fine."

"That's what Kristine keeps saying."

I smile at her grimacing face. "Just think about how great it's going to be once you get there."

"Well, that's the problem, isn't it? Getting there."

I change the subject. "So, what states are you going to visit?"

"Massachusetts, New Hampshire, Vermont, and New York."

"Wow."

"I think we're even going over to see Niagara Falls."

There is genuine excitement in her voice. I make a mental promise that I will go on adventures well into my eighties, even if I have to navigate from a wheelchair.

"It sounds wonderful, Ladora."

"I hope so. You like to travel?"

"I love to travel." I think of trips with the kids, trips with my hubby, trips with friends. And even if it's only an outing into the woods, sitting around a campfire and eating hobo stew, the memories are irreplaceable.

"It's just too bad the big-ticket items are so far away,"

Ladora says.

"Right. Wouldn't it be great if we could hop on a bus to London?"

"Or Hawaii?" Her eyes linger on her photo of Waikiki Beach.

"Yeah."

"'Course the airline people wouldn't be happy."

"True." Looking at the time on the kitty clock, I jump. "Hey, I'd better be going!"

Ladora laughs. "Lost track of time, did ya?"

"I did. See you next Thursday." I grab the food baskets and head for the door.

"Want to borrow my jogging outfit?"

"Next time!"

I'm out the door and power-walking down the hallway. Actually, power-walking for all of ten seconds, then the heat stops me short and I stand gasping for breathable air. I think of Lucille and Betty in their squashed little duplex, and I trudge ahead. I hope the thermos container is keeping their lunches cold.

I pull up in front of the faded house and take a deep breath. *I can do this.* I turn off the engine and jump out into the stifling summer heat. My fingers feel like little sausages stuck onto my hands, and I berate myself for not drinking more water. Great. Watch me keel over from heat exhaustion on Lucille's front steps. I gather the lunches, tuck the newspaper under my arm, and head for the house. I hear the old window air conditioner wheezing cool air into the front room. It sounds like it will breathe its last any second, as brackish water drips from its insides onto the sidewalk.

Just as I come to the front steps, I look down at my feet and realize I'm about to step into a patch of dried blood. I try to force my mind to think it's something else, but the evidence is unmistakable. I'm going into panic mode when Lucille yanks open the door.

"What are you staring at?"

She looks like an angry dog that's been kicked too many times.

"I—I'm—is that blood, Lucille?"

"Yeah. So?"

"Did somebody get hurt?" I can see the pain behind her defiance.

"Sorry old fool. He knows he can't drink. Not the hard stuff." I assume she's talking about Marv. "I'm gonna kill that nephew of mine. Takes him out drinking, and then just dumps him out of the car at 2 a.m. Idiot tries to get up the steps and falls smack down on his head."

Lucille is a very stoic woman, and I can't imagine the pain she's feeling to gush out this many words at once.

"Is he okay?"

I move up onto the landing, and she opens the screen door. The smell from inside the house is so putrid I have to force myself not to retch.

"He can go to the devil for all I care."

Betty jerks so violently in her bed that she knocks one of her pillows into a lamp, which then crashes onto the floor.

"Oh, crap!" Lucille rushes to her. "It's okay. It's okay, baby."

I step onto the threshold of the house. "Can I help, Lucille?"

The Route

I put my hand up over my mouth.

"No! No, it's okay. Just stay back there!"

The room is dim, but I can see Betty's face clearly as Lucille attempts to calm her down and reposition her on the bed. High on Betty's right cheekbone is a vivid purple bruise. Her eye is swollen and bloodshot. I move forward a few steps and then stand frozen in place. *Marv hit her.*

Lucille hisses at me. "Just go outside."

I turn and move back out onto the landing. *He hit her.*

Lucille finally comes back to the door. "Give me the lunch," she growls.

I turn around and hand over the sandwiches, cold peaches, milk, and newspaper. "Is Betty okay?"

I can tell Lucille wants to say, "None of your meddling business," but instead she pushes her gray hair out of her face and lies. "She got upset last night. Poor baby doesn't like it when her daddy and I fight. She got so upset she broke a blood vessel in her face."

"Oh." I try to mask the disbelief in my eyes.

"Yeah. She'll be all right," Lucille insists.

"A blood vessel?"

"Yeah." She glares at me defensively. "I kicked her daddy out, so she'll calm down now."

"Does she need to see—"

The door closes in my face.

"—a doctor?" The empty basket feels like a ten-pound weight at the end of my arm.

I don't know if I can do this anymore. I'm sickened by the violence. I step around the dried blood and head for the SUV,

115

fighting the overwhelming impulse to scream or cry or be sick. Life is not supposed to be like this! I throw the basket into the vehicle and slam the door. I head to Joyce's praying that I can make some sort of sense of all this pain and mess, but my mind is caught in the sour images, and I find that my mantra has failed me. I am so angry! I'm angry at stupid drinkers and drug users that go around ruining everybody else's lives! I'm angry at my son! I cry—hard. I'm angry at myself for being angry at my son. I see him little and innocent: playing T ball, or finger painting, or making something amazing with Legos. I grab a tissue out of my purse and blow my nose. Maybe I'll find an Al-Anon meeting after I'm done with deliveries. That's the ticket. Find a meeting and dump out some of this anger and pain.

I stand on Joyce's front porch, hesitating to knock. My hands are shaking, and even in the heat I feel clammy. I used to love coming to this house. Joyce was bright and funny, her caustic wit so refreshing, but now . . .

Alex has moved her bed from the upstairs bedroom to the front room on the main floor. Joyce can no longer climb stairs, or go outside, or talk. She struggles to get from her place at the kitchen table to the toilet. She needs the support of her family, but her second husband, Jack, died two years ago, she never had any children, and her younger sister from California is in ill health and can't come to care for her.

Alex has tried to get her into a facility, but Joyce is adamant about not leaving her home. A hospice nurse comes once a day to check on her and administer meds.

Alex says that the CEO of the tobacco company might as well come and wrap his fingers around Joyce's throat and strangle her to death. At least that way she wouldn't suffer these weeks and months of slow suffocation.

I'm stunned by all of it. My grandpa was a smoker, but I was too little to understand the consequences of the choices he made, or why my Nana would get so upset when Grandpa would take off his oxygen support and shuffle outside for a cigarette. And I wasn't born when my other grandpa died of lung cancer in our home.

I stand with my fist pressed against the door. *How can I do this?* I force myself to knock, then open the door. *Dear Lord, please give me strength to just make it through this day.*

"Hi, Joyce! It's Carol." I move into the front room knowing she won't answer. She is lying in her bed, propped up in a semi-sitting position. I move to her and find her awake.

"Hi, Joyce."

She smiles.

"Do you feel like eating?"

She shakes her head.

"I'll just put it in the refrigerator."

She gives me another weak smile.

When I come back, she points to her front door.

"You want me to leave?"

Looking sad, she shakes her head and whispers, "Mail."

"You want me to see if the mail's here?"

She nods. I go to her front porch and check the mailbox. I take out a coupon booklet, an AARP announcement, and a letter from California. I return to her bedside.

"A letter from California."

Her face brightens and she indicates that I should open it.

I hand her the opened envelope. "Here you go."

She pushes it back to me.

"You want me to read it?"

She nods.

On the outside of the card is a darling little boy with a triple-decker ice cream cone.

I read. "I heard you were sick, so I wanted to send something to cheer you up."

I open the card. Inside is a picture of a gorgeous hunk in the smallest Speedo swimsuit one can imagine.

Joyce and I start laughing. How can we be doing this? She can't laugh, and I don't feel like laughing, but we're doing it anyway. Then Joyce moans and rolls over on her side, unable to breathe. I don't know what to do. I'm trying to find the phone to call 911, when Alex comes in through the front door.

"Alex, help!"

He moves quickly but calmly to the bed.

"What's up?" he asks in a low tone.

"We were laughing, and now she can't breathe."

He sits on the side of the bed rubbing Joyce's back with one hand and getting the oxygen mask with the other. Joyce grips onto his shirt, her eyes full of panic and pain.

"It's okay, Joyce. Relax. It's okay. Let this work for you."

I watch as Joyce's body reacts to his words and touch.

I feel terrible. "I'm sorry. She wanted me to read her this card from California."

"It's okay. It's okay." I'm not sure if he's talking to me or Joyce, but I take solace anyway. Joyce is relaxing and breathing under Alex's touch—and the oxygen mask.

The Route

I feel lightheaded, so I sit down in a worn leather chair. Alex looks over at me. "You okay?"

"Woozy."

"Well, sit still. I don't have another oxygen mask."

"Very funny. I'll be fine. How's Joyce doing?"

"Good." He smiles at her. "She's tough." Tears well up in Joyce's eyes. "I know, Duchess. It's hard isn't it? Just relax. It's okay, we're right here with you." Slowly her eyes close. Alex catches the startled look on my face. "She's sleeping."

It takes every ounce of strength I have to stand up. "I'd better be going." I move to Joyce and run my hand softly over her hair. I want her to tell me a political joke. I want to tease her about Alex. I want her not to be in so much pain.

Alex picks up my basket. "I'll walk you to the door."

"It's okay, I..."

He puts his warm hand on the small of my back, and I shut up. What a comforting feeling—no innuendo, no selfish motives, just genuine compassion. Whoever has this man for a friend is extremely lucky.

"Thanks, Alex."

He opens the door for me and hands me the basket. "Is the grouchy lady next?"

"She is."

He winks at me. "You can do it."

I want to put my head on his chest and cry for about an hour, but instead I turn and head for my vehicle. *One more stop. I can make it through one more stop.* Why does Viola have to be at the end of the route? I need a smiling, optimistic person to cheer me up. Well, maybe she'll have her bra and panties out on the fence again, or maybe she won't be home. But she's always home. I drive to her trailer on automatic pilot.

I'm thinking about the conversation I'll be having with Valerie later this afternoon—reporting Marv's abuse of Betty, informing her about Joyce's condition, and explaining why I'm dropping out of the program. *Am I? Should I toss a coin?*

A memory keeps popping into my head, of the time my dog Tuffy got a hold of my faded rag doll, Emily Ann. The stupid mutt ran down the block shaking his head back and forth, causing poor Emily Ann's arms and legs to flop around like, well, a rag doll. Right now I feel like Emily Ann, and all I want is for the thrashing to stop.

I decide to let fate have a hand in my decision. If I get to Viola's and she's nice, I'll stay on, but if she's cranky, I'll turn in my baskets and my badge. I take a deep breath, feeling as if the outcome is pretty much sealed.

When I arrive at Viola's trailer, I'm so much more than two minutes late. She's not out on her stoop, which is unusual. Maybe she's inside wolfing down crackers, or attempting to escape the afternoon heat. Then again, her metal trailer could be like a toaster oven, which, of course, would turn the hungry little woman into the Wicked Witch from *The Wizard of Oz*. I look down at my volunteer badge and bid it a fond farewell.

I load up Viola's lunch—with no extras-for-niceness incentives—and head for the trailer. As I reach the stoop, I hear the faint hum of a very efficient air conditioner. Well, so much for the heat theory. I'm still a good twenty minutes late, though, which certainly warrants a good tongue-lashing.

I knock, and during the wait, I anticipate what wondrous

The Route

Phyllis Diller outfit Viola will have on today. It will be my final fashion show. The door opens onto Levis and a denim shirt worn by a smiling, big-boned woman of forty who is definitely not Viola.

"Hi. Can I help you?" the woman asks politely.

I can't answer. *Is this some sort of trick?*

Viola's voice comes from the darkness. "Who is it, Pat?"

"Don't know. Some lady with a basket."

"I'm delivering Viola's lunch."

Viola comes to the door. "Is that my lunch girl?"

"Hi, Viola. Sorry, I'm—"

"Well, isn't this nice. This is my niece, Pat, and I've forgotten your name."

"Carol."

"Pat, this is Carol."

"Hi."

"Hi."

"I guess we don't need the lunch today," Viola chirps. "Pat made me a delicious tuna sandwich."

"Tuna?"

"With a cottage-cheese-and-tomato salad."

"Salad?" I stand staring at Pat like a deer in the headlights.

Pat frowns at me. "Are you all right? Would you like a drink of water or something?"

"Water? No, no, I'm fine, thank you." I get a grip on myself. "So, Viola, would you like to keep the meal for your dinner?"

"Could I do that?"

"Sure."

"Well, I'd like to, yes. Isn't that nice, Pat? I've told you how nice these people are to me."

Okay, Fate, shut up! You don't need to knock me over the head. I hand over Viola's dinner, smile at Pat, and stumble back to my vehicle in a total stupor. Maybe the volunteer pool is so drought-stricken that Fate needs every halfway willing Joe—no matter how pitiful. Yeah, pitiful, that's me all right.

I crawl into the SUV, turn on the air conditioning, lean my head against the steering wheel, and cry.

I need a two-week vacation.

CHAPTER 7

The Long and Winding Road

A week after the card-from-California day, I show up on Joyce's doorstep with boneless baked chicken, Tater Tots, fruit cocktail, and a banana. I knock and try to open the door, but it's locked. I stand for a moment, wondering what to do. I try the door again. Locked? The door has never been locked.

A voice calls from behind me. "Hey! Can I help you?"

I turn and see a young woman coming across the street. She's carrying a baby and looking at me as if I'm a door-to-door salesman. Her short hair is spiky and an unrealistic shade of black. She comes into Joyce's yard like she owns it.

"Do you want something?" she snaps.

She looks to be fifteen, and her attitude makes the hair on my neck stand up.

"No. I have Joyce's meal, but her door is . . ."

"Didn't someone call you?"

"No. What do you mean?"

"That lady died last night."

"What?"

"About six."

"Oh." I clamp down on my emotions. I am not going to cry in front of this indifferent stranger. *That lady?* I just want this uncaring teenager and her baby to go away. "Are you a neighbor?" I ask.

"Yeah, I live over there." She points at the squalid little hut across the street.

"Did you know Joyce?" I ask.

"Who? Oh, was that her name? No, I didn't know her. She was old."

I want to snap off a few acidic remarks, but I need information, so I grit my teeth and take a deep breath. "Was she alone when she died?"

The girl looks like she's trying to figure out an algebra problem. "Alone?"

"Was anyone with her?"

"Oh. I think that nurse lady was."

"The hospice nurse?"

"I guess. She comes every day. I was out starting the barbeque. Pretty soon after, that cute guy showed up."

I feel tears pressing against the back of my eyes. Alex was with her. I can see him sitting close to Joyce on the bed, gently rubbing her back and whispering words of comfort in his soft, mellow voice.

"It's okay, Duchess, I'm right here. It's okay. You can let go now. You learned a lot of important stuff while you were here, and you were always good to other people. You can take that with you."

"Is that guy her grandson? Man, he is so buff."

I want this youngster to stop talking and go away.

She shifts the baby to the other hip. "About a half hour later, an ambulance came rolling in. No siren or anything. They brought her out on one of those . . ."

"Okay. Thanks." I turn to leave.

"Do you know what they're gonna do with the house?"

Did hyenas raise this girl? I turn back to her. "Excuse me?"

"The house. Are they gonna sell it or what?"

"I don't know, and it's not an appropriate question."

"What?"

"It's not something you should be asking."

"Oh." Seeing her face flush, I restrain my anger. After all, no one hired me to be this girl's teacher, and it's not her fault that she had a dolt for a mother.

I try to steady my breathing before I speak. "I'm sorry. I'm just upset about Joyce's death. She—she was my friend, and a fascinating woman."

"Really? I never saw her come out of her house."

"Well, she had a whole amazing lifetime before she went in there."

The girl looks at me blankly like I'm speaking Greek, and the baby coughs and sneezes.

"She was an army nurse during World War II, stationed in the Philippines."

"Yeah?" She wipes the baby's nose with her shirt. I bet she's never heard of the Philippines or World War II.

"Joyce took care of a lot of wounded soldiers, and she was nearly captured by the Japanese. She saved a lot of the hospital staff."

"Hmm."

I can see that my tale is not captivating the heart and soul of this self-absorbed young woman. I move back to Joyce's house and put my hand on her door.

"Nobody's in there."

"I know. I'm just saying good-bye."

I hear her mumble, "Weird," but I let it slide. I'm too caught up in my own sadness to worry about this girl's emotional handicaps. I say a little prayer for Joyce and head for the SUV. I wish Alex were here. We could sit on the front steps together and share stories about Joyce's life. We could miss her and retell her funny jokes. But life moves on, and I have Viola waiting on her stoop. The girl follows me out of the yard.

"I'm sorry about your friend dying."

A shudder of tears runs through me. "Thanks."

The baby starts to fuss, and the girl turns and walks back across the street.

I stand at the SUV unwilling to open the door—just letting the warmth of the sun soak into my skin.

Death isn't something most people spend time thinking about. Car payments, buying stuff, where to eat lunch, pain—these things occupy our time, but death, no. We are too immersed in the day-to-day to worry about our non-existence, and maybe it's supposed to be like that. Maybe death is meant to stay out of our way until its presence requires reflection, because when death sits down in our living rooms, we have to stop and confront the huge aspects of life. Is there something after the shutting down of bodily functions? If there is something, what? If there isn't something, why not? What happens to the joy, love, and learning we acquire? Should I be worried if I'm a rotten person? Will we be ourselves on the other side and have association with family and friends, or are they lost to us forever? I evaluate the doctrines of spirituality that have comforted and informed me all my life, and a little ray of surety breaks into my thinking.

I open the vehicle door, throw the basket into the passenger's side, and climb in. Numbly, I start the engine and turn on the air-conditioning. I take one more long look at the white house with the brown shutters. Everything looks the same. I find that odd.

~

In September, Ladora went to the Northeast with her family, and came back with pictures of herself standing in groves of autumn brilliance, eating lobster with a big bib around her neck, and pretending to dive into Niagara Falls. She survived the plane trip, but said she was glad for the extra protective underwear they have for seniors.

Kristine took the photo of her mom pretending to be Sonia Heni at Niagara Falls, and had it enlarged to an 8x10 and framed in rosewood. Ladora put it on the wall, right between her pictures of the Bavarian Alps and Waikiki.

Upon returning from her adventure, Ladora promptly took her rolls of film to the one-hour developer, secured the finished treasures in a small photo album, and placed the book prominently on her bookshelf. The mementoes were fodder for lunchtime conversation.

"So, this is Kristine's husband?" I ask, pointing at a rugged-looking man in a rugby shirt and jeans.

Ladora stops eating and looks over. "Yep. Norman. Very smart."

"Architect?"

"Vet."

"Really?"

"Yeah."

I think of poor little Buffy, Viola's mangy Methuselah dog.

"Boy, I sure could have used him one time." I turn the page of the album and see a picture of three kids tossing autumn leaves at each other. "And these are your grandchildren?"

"Yep. Megan, Chloe, and Trevor. Real fancy-pants names, huh? But they're good kids. That little Trevor had us in stitches the whole trip."

"How old is he?"

"Four. And the girls are nine and seven." Ladora chuckles. "Only reason I remember their ages is because Megan kept telling me."

"Precocious?"

"Let's just say she's her mother all over again. Chloe's kinda quiet, and Trevor . . ." She shakes her head and chuckles again. "One day we stopped for burgers and milk shakes. Well, little guy wanted his own chocolate milk shake, and he didn't want the straw or the lid. So, he's got the cup tipped up, and this thick milk shake just dumps all over his face. All you could see for a second were his little eyes blinking." Landor is back at the Burger Barn in Woodford Hallow, Vermont, laughing with her family at the delight of life.

I turn the page onto more beautiful scenes. "This countryside is amazing, Ladora."

"Most beautiful thing I've ever seen. You can't even imagine there could be colors like that."

I smile at the enthusiasm in her voice. "And everybody survived traveling together?"

"Well, they got kinda tired of me asking when we were gonna get someplace, but other than that we did fine."

I chuckle as I turn pages. "I'd love to visit that part of the country."

"Haven't you ever been there?"

"Niagara Falls when I was eight. I don't remember much."

"Well, you have to go back!" Landora insists.

"Oh, I couldn't!"

"Why not?"

"I'd have to get on an airplane!"

She socks me on the arm. "You are not funny. Anyway, you could wear those diaper underwear."

We laugh together like school chums.

"I'd better go."

"Well, if you gotta go, you gotta go."

We laugh again. Toilet jokes. Fifty years old and seventy-five years old, and we're still laughing at toilet jokes.

I pick up my basket. "I'll see you next Thursday, Miss Ladora."

"Who knows? I may be in Hawaii!"

I smile and step out into the hallway.

Who knows, indeed?

CHAPTER 8

Side Streets

None of my people dressed up for Halloween. I thought Mary might put on a Richard Nixon mask, or Bea might wear a crown, or Maxine might pretend to be Barbara Bush, but, to a person, they seemed content to let the ghoul's holiday pass away without a scream. I thought about putting on roller blades and pretending to be a carhop, but I didn't relish taking a trip to the emergency room, or dumping my people's lunches onto the floor. I'd built up a reputation for being semi-reliable, which I didn't want to jeopardize for the sake of possible slight applause.

As I place turkey goulash, rice, cooked carrots, and a banana into the basket for Goldie, I think about the transformation my route has gone through over the past year—LaRue, Elaine, and Olea are in special-care facilities; Joyce is amusing St. Peter at the Pearly Gates; and three new names have magically appeared on my papers. Russell has joined the Maple Leaf gang, Althia lives in her own little cottage, and Elsie resides in a mini-condo. Valerie has also written me a note stating that the meal routes might be changing again, with Lucille and Betty assigned to a different driver. I'll wait and see.

Goldie is still with us, but she seems more fragile as each Thursday goes by, her body losing connection with food and time. I care about all the wondrous people on my route, but I have to admit a special affinity for Goldie, maybe because she was my first delivery, or maybe because she always makes me feel good about myself, like I can make it through any challenge life might throw at me. I've learned so much from her about accepting life on life's terms and letting go of things over which I have no control. *God has no grandchildren*—it's become my favorite thought for the day.

As I drive to Goldie's home, I pass an assortment of brides, ghosts, vampires, and Barbies on their way to afternoon kindergarten. A very large child in a pirate costume escorts them, and I'm hoping he's one of the tots' fathers and not some poor kid who's been held back too many times.

I push the doorbell, knowing that Goldie will not be the one opening the door.

"Hi, Carol!"

"Hi, Janet. Is she asleep or awake today?"

"Actually, she's awake. She's out on the patio. Robert's with her."

It's good to know that she's up and about. "Could I go say hi?"

"Absolutely. I'll put the stuff away while you visit."

I set all the food on the table and move to the back door. I find Goldie sitting in a lawn chair, bundled in a plaid flannel comforter, while Robert sits behind her on the picnic bench, brushing her hair. I start to step back into the house, not wanting to intrude on such tenderness, but Robert catches the movement and looks over at me.

"Hey, it's the lunch lady! Come on over."

I move to Goldie's side. She looks up at me and smiles.

"Hello, my dear."

Even on this chilly afternoon her warmth radiates through my clothes and skin, right into my heart. I look at Robert, who smiles understandingly. He's felt that sunny encouragement his entire life. What a fortunate fellow.

I sit down on the bench. "So, who's your cute hairdresser?"

"What?"

Her hearing has diminished because of the strokes she's suffered, so I speak louder and point to Robert. "Your cute hairdresser."

She nods. "That's my son, Robert. He's doing my hair.

"Nice."

"What?"

I give her the thumbs-up sign.

Goldie smiles and nods. "Does it look okay?"

I nod.

She smiles. "He's good to me."

"He is."

"What?"

I speak louder. "He's a good man."

"Yes, he is. He is."

Robert leans close to his mother's ear. "Don't embarrass me, now."

She chuckles.

I sit quietly for a moment watching Robert carefully braid his mother's hair. I feel that tender grip around my heart that signals a certain flood of tears. I take a deep breath and stand. "Well, I'd better get going, hungry folks to feed."

The Route

Robert laughs softly. "Yep, nothing worse than hungry seniors."

I pat Goldie on the back. "I just wanted to say hi."

"What?"

"I'm going now!" I wave and Goldie waves back.

"Bye-bye, Hazel!"

Robert looks up at me. "Hazel? I didn't think your name was Hazel."

"It's not, it's Carol, but she's been calling me Hazel the last little while."

"That was her sister's name. My aunt Hazel."

"I see."

Robert pats his mother's head gently. "She's been missing people. A while ago it was her mom and dad. Now, it must be Aunt Hazel. Sorry she called you the wrong name."

"No, that's fine. Actually, I feel complimented."

Robert shrugs and shakes his head "I don't know, Aunt Hazel was pretty weird."

I laugh. "Oh, no! My secret's out!"

Robert smiles at me. "Yeah, you are like Hazel."

"Whoever I am, I'd better get going. Nice seeing you again, Robert."

"You too, Carol. Thanks for bringing my mom's lunch."

I've been around men who vacation in the Bahamas, eat fifty-dollar business lunches, and wear eight-hundred-dollar suits, who have far less class than this auto mechanic in Levi's.

I leave the twosome sharing contented respect in the cool autumn sunshine. I walk into the house, gather my basket, say good-bye to Janet, and head for my vehicle. I feel calm and in balance—probably what those yoga people feel after an hour on their heads. I don't know if I could ever talk my body into those contortions, but I figure a little more time for peaceful meditation would do me a world of good. I wonder if one can achieve enlightenment chanting *Om* on an exercise machine.

As I drive to the apartment building, I pop in my CD of show tunes. I'm partial to *Oliver* and *The Sound of Music*. I try to recall if any of my folks are music buffs; Maxine is the only one I can think of, and she likes all kinds of music, with classical at the top of her list. Tom reads his Chinese newspaper; Mary watches the History Channel, movies, and CNN; Bea likes soap operas; Ladora has discovered travel videos, and of course, Marcus the exercise guy. Now, Lucille and Betty have the TV on all day, every day. Betty especially likes game shows. And as for Viola, I have no idea how she gets through her day, as I've never been inside her trailer. She probably spends a lot of time incanting, and mixing potions.

I knock on Tom's door.

"Ah! Come in, come in!"

I step into the dim apartment and call out a Chinese greeting. "Ni hao!"

Tom is delighted. "Oh! Ni hao, ni hao. You speak Chinese!"

"Well, one word."

"Is very good."

"Thank you."

He becomes my teacher. "Sye sye. It means thank you."

"Sye sye."

"Yes. Good."

The Route

He stands by me in the kitchen as I set out his lunch. He points at the goulash.

"What is that?"

"Goulash," I answer, trying to make my voice deep and shaky. "Does it look scary?"

"Scary?" He laughs. "No, but you are scary."

"Thank you," I answer in my best Bela Lugosi impression.

"So, what is it?" he asks again.

"Well, it's something made with turkey. They're just calling it goulash because of Halloween."

He stands staring at me a moment, then laughs. "Ah, goulash. Goulash. I get it. It does not look so tasty, but I will try. Rice is good, and banana."

I set my basket on the counter. "Was your wife May a good cook?"

"May? Cook? Oh, very good cook. Seventy years married."

"I know. That's amazing."

"Amazing." He walks over to the family photo, and I follow. "This is May and seven children. All good children."

I think about Mei Ping and his family escaping Mainland China—their flight to Taiwan. I think about them coming to America, and I wonder if Tom still dreams in Chinese or if he hears his mother's voice, *"Mei Ping, do not worry about me. You must go and build a new life. Take your family and find peace."*

Tom is pointing at his children. "All good children. They all respect mother."

"That's nice."

"Yes, nice. They no respect, she hit with broom."

We laugh together.

"Good for her."

"Girls never get broom, but boys . . . she chase them all around." He imitates May. *"Stand still, demon boys, so I can whack you with broom! Drive out evil spirit!"*

I smile at his antics, wondering if it's the truth or only a story.

"I miss her," he says, touching the glass over her image.

"Of course. She was your best friend."

"Best friend." He looks tenderly at the photo, and I think of seventy years of loving commitment. Only a few couples are lucky enough to be in a relationship where both parties are willing to be selfless, thinking first of the happiness of the other. In the intricate game of marriage, each party has to play fairly, or no one wins.

"You're a lucky man, Mr. Tom."

He smiles. "Very lucky. Married on thirteenth day. Very lucky."

"Well, I'd better be going," I say reluctantly.

"Ah, I have something for you."

We're not supposed to take gifts from our people . . .

"You like chocolate?"

. . . but, in this case . . .

"I do."

He goes to his cupboard and brings out a box of Godiva chocolates! I'm stunned. Here I was, expecting a box of cheap, leftover chocolates from Easter—not that I wouldn't have accepted cheap Easter chocolates, as I've certainly been known to slurp Hershey's chocolate syrup right out of the plastic jug, but to be offered chocolate heaven, well, one lights a candle.

Tom notices me staring at the box and not moving. "You no like this?"

"What? Are you kidding? This stuff is great!"

He chuckles at my enthusiasm. "Have two."

"Really?" I feel like I did when I was out trick or treating and somebody gave me a full-sized 3 Musketeers bar. I carefully choose two beautifully decorated chocolates. "Thank you so much."

"I get you baggie to put them in." He goes to a neatly organized drawer and pulls out a plastic bag for my treasures.

"You're a prince. Shar shar."

He corrects me. "Sye sye."

"Oh! Sye sye. Sorry."

"No, you learning. Is good. Makes me feel your caring for me." He smiles and opens the door. I hug him gently and step into the hallway.

"See you next Thursday," I say, holding the bag of chocolates over my heart.

"Right. Thursday. Okay." He smiles broadly and shuts the door.

I whistle as I head off to Mary's, wondering if I'll see her today. The county's assigned her a senior companion, and the woman comes three times a week, taking Mary grocery shopping, to doctor's appointments, and sometimes just plain joyriding. I have a feeling Mary doesn't mind missing television all that much.

She happens to be home today, and Gracie—the

companion—isn't with her.

"Come in! Come in!" Mary calls happily. "I haven't seen you for a while."

"I know. You've been off gallivanting."

"Eye doctor."

"Well, that's not gallivanting."

She sighs. "Tell me about it."

"Everything okay?"

"I'm gonna get that operation."

"Which one?"

"That one that helps you see better. I'll still have to wear glasses, but just regular ones."

"That's good, isn't it?"

"Is it? Good gravy, I don't want nobody pokin' around in my eyes."

"Yeah, I can understand that."

"Jonathan says I should go for it. Of course he can say that—they're not his eyeballs."

Mary's grandson Jonathan is often a topic of conversation between us. It's a woman thing, spending lots of time talking about our families and trying to figure out how to solve all their problems. "How's he doing?"

"Better. Likes his apartment. He and his girlfriend broke up, and that's too bad, 'cause she's good for him. Keeps him in line."

"Any more trouble with his dad?"

"I don't know. Bill's taken off for Arizona. Some big-shot deal. I don't know." Her eyes fill with tears and she looks out the window. "I just wish he could get himself sober."

"Yeah." I think of my boy and his attempts to get sober. He hasn't quite caught the vision of his powerlessness, still struggling along the road of pride. For some reason the idea of "I can't, God can, I think I'll let Him" eludes him.

I make a check of Mary's lunch items. "Well, you're all set."

"Thanks, sweetie."

I move to the door. "When do you decide about your operation?"

"Monday."

"Okay. I'll check with you next Thursday, then."

"Okay." There is acute sadness in her voice.

I close the door and look around for something to kick. I'd kick Bill if I could find him. Bill is one of those selfish people who thinks his actions make no impact on the lives of other people—or, even worse, knows his actions make an impact, and could care less.

I move quickly toward the quiet elegance of Bea's antique haven and am surprised to find her home. Today should be a beauty-parlor day.

"Hello! Come in! The door's open."

I move into the dim apartment. "Bea?"

"Hello! Come in!" She turns on her small lamp.

I move into her living room. "Hi, Bea. Were you napping?"

"I was, but it's fine. Come in, come in. I can nap anytime."

I notice that her hair is flat and the color drab. "I'm surprised to find you home."

Her hand goes immediately to her hair, and I feel terrible for having alluded to her skipped beauty date.

"I had to miss my appointment. I wasn't feeling well this morning."

"I'm sorry."

"Oh, I'm much better now. I was just tired. Rita's going to slip me in on Friday." She turns off the television. "So, you brought my lunch. Wonderful."

I take out a polished cotton place mat, lay it on the table, and start arranging her lunch items on top. Somehow, the microwaveable cardboard container looks foolish sitting there, as does the milk carton and banana. What should be sitting there instead is Waldorf salad, baked salmon puff, and a thin slice of raspberry cheesecake.

"Now, doesn't that look good?" Bea's voice brings me back to the rice and cooked carrots. "Is it turkey divan?"

"Well, they're calling it goulash."

"Goulash? Oh, how funny. Turkey goulash. Even better."

Bea has eaten in great restaurants all around the world, and yet she's happy about tepid turkey goulash in a cardboard container? That's the true definition of gratitude.

"What's your favorite food, Bea?"

"Favorite? I don't know if I have a favorite. Randy and I liked just about everything. We loved the German food—those wonderful sausages, or thin slices of sautéed meat, with gravy, dumplings, and white asparagus." She's sitting somewhere in the Bavarian Alps, eating a scrumptious dinner and watching the sunset. "I've had a very good life."

Gratitude.

The Route

She tucks a napkin into the neck of her blouse. "What about you? What is your favorite food?"

"Anything someone else cooks," I respond, and Bea smiles.

"Well, I think you're all set."

"Thank you so much, Carol. And thank you for the nice visit."

I make a mental note to myself: be grateful—even for life's smallest gifts.

"I'll see you next Thursday, Bea."

"I'll be looking forward to it." I open the door and she calls after me, "Oh, watch out for little ghosts and goblins!"

"I will."

"Goulash," I hear her chuckle as I close the door.

Such a dear woman. You'd think her daughter would care as well for her mom as she does for her mom's antiques. I scold myself for judging a situation I know only a little about. As my dad would say, "Take care of your own lawn before you mow the neighbor's."

The hallway is chilly, and I move off quickly for Maxine's. She'll be home. She has been home every Thursday for the past two months, because she's been diagnosed with leukemia and has been undergoing radiation and cycles of chemotherapy. Her beautiful white hair is gone, and chemo sores are beginning to form inside her mouth. Because of the sores, her meals must be specially prepared and puréed. She rarely eats the food, preferring instead to drink the energy shakes also provided by the meals program. I stand in front of her apartment, tear open a disinfecting hand towelette, and wash my hands. I gently open her door without knocking.

"Beth? Maxine?" I expect to hear Beth's voice, but Maxine calls back.

"Come on in. Is it the lunch lady?"

"It is. It's Carol." The apartment is dim and filled with soft instrumental music.

"Would you please put it in the refrigerator?" she asks politely.

"Of course," I answer. I deposit the meal in the Amana and go in to see Maxine.

The drapes are drawn back just enough to illuminate the couch where she's lying. When my eyes adjust, I can see that she's wearing a really ugly hat. She smiles and motions me closer.

"Do you have time to sit?"

"Of course." I sit down in a chair that's been pulled up beside the couch. "Where's Beth?"

"Grocery shopping."

I'm shocked. "She drove herself to the store?"

"Heavens no." Maxine smiles weakly. "Could you imagine that disaster?"

"Actually, I can imagine, and it isn't pretty."

"No, no. She took that special senior's bus."

"Oh, good." I shift in my seat, wondering what I should say now.

There is a long silence, and since Maxine's eyes are closed, I figure she's fallen asleep. Then, she whispers softly, "Carol?"

"Yes?"

"Do you believe in spiritual things?"

"I . . . what do you mean?"

"Life after this one, heaven, ghosts."

Hmm. Not your regular small talk. "Well, I try to keep an open mind. I don't know about ghosts, but I do think there is a heaven."

"An actual place?"

"Yep."

"With people we've loved?"

I nod. "And animals. It wouldn't be heaven without animals."

"And hair?"

I chuckle at her resilience. "Yep. Any color you want."

"I've always wanted to be a redhead," she confesses.

"And you get to have your best body back—a perfect body."

"Young?"

"Prime of life."

Maxine goes very quiet. "Carol?"

"Yes?"

"I loved my husband."

"I know you did."

"He's been gone twenty-three years."

"I know."

"And I've loved him all that time. William was my sweetheart, my dearest friend."

I sit quietly, listening to the quality of her voice. It's as if she's speaking from far away.

"I've had a recurring dream, and I've never experienced anything like it." She pauses. "Would you like to hear it?"

I nod.

"I'm in this beautiful place—a garden—and the trees have

this golden shimmer, and the flowers are amazing, all different colors on one stem." She stops for a moment and points to her side table. "Would you hand me some ice chips, please?"

Every morning, the first thing Beth does in caring for her friend is to crunch up a bunch of ice and put it into an insulated bucket on the side table. Maxine closes her eyes and lets the ice melt slowly in her mouth.

"I see someone walking towards me from a distance. I know right away it's William, and I run toward him. I'm running! It's the most amazing feeling. I haven't run in years. When I get to William, he smiles at me, and . . . he's young! He's in his twenties, but it's my William. He takes my hand and we walk together, all over the place. I—I don't know how to explain this, but . . ." She looks at me warily. "I feel like I'm actually there—like it's not a dream. Beth says I'm loony, that of course it's a dream, but what do you think?"

I reflect on the steady, unpretentious nature of Maxine's personality. "I don't think you're loony."

"You don't?"

"No."

"Maybe it's all the treatment and medication," she says soberly.

I take her hand. "Maybe, and maybe it isn't. Who am I to say? I felt my dad's presence very strongly for weeks after he died."

"Really?" Maxine closes her eyes, and tears squeeze out from under her eyelids. "It's so comforting to me. I have no fear at all about going to that place."

The door opens and Beth comes in. She's wearing a hospital

The Route

mask and carrying two plastic grocery bags. She sets the bags on the counter, unsuccessfully trying to be quiet. She shushes the grocery bags.

I look over at Maxine and she's smiling. She whispers. "Uh-oh. We'd better be on our best behavior." I nod, and she reaches over and rests her fingers lightly on my arm. "Thank you for listening."

Beth comes tiptoeing into the room. She sees me and comes to my side, looking down at Maxine with a protective air.

"You awake?" Maxine nods, and Beth turns her eagle eyes on me. "You'd better not be sick, holding her hand like that. You aren't, are ya?"

I feel like I'm six and full of germs. "No. I'm not sick. I've never felt better."

"Okay, then. How about a shake?"

"Sure!" I answer brightly.

Beth whacks me. "Not you, goofball."

Maxine smiles. "I'd love a shake, you tyrant."

"Okay, then!" Beth barks, moving back into the kitchen. "Somebody's got to keep order in this place."

Maxine and I share a look of delight.

"My Beth is quite a character."

"I heard that!"

"And ears like a fox."

I stand and pick up my basket, keeping a tight hold on my emotions. "See you next Thursday."

"Okay."

I walk to the door. "'Bye, Miss Beth."

She looks up from her work and smiles. "Don't get lost."

"I'll try not to." I move quickly out the door as tears run down my cheeks.

Don't get lost. Life is such an amazing and scary road we all have to travel. Who would think of trying to walk it alone, or for any reason making the path more difficult? There are certainly enough ruts, rocks, and landslides along the way, without us adding potholes.

I fish a tissue out of my pocket and am blowing my nose when the apartment manager, with her clipboard, comes around the corner of the hallway. Her eyes dart to my reddened face and then back down to her clipboard as she passes me with a terse smile and no greeting. I shove the tissue back into my pocket. She must think I'm a nut case, because every time she sees me I'm either smiling like a tippler or crying like a mutt. Luckily, Ladora is next, and she accepts me any way I am. I knock on her door and am chagrined when it opens.

"Kristine! Hi!" I feel like a mud rat.

"Hi, Carol. Please come in." How can she be so elegant wearing a clunky plastic apron and latex gloves?

Ladora calls to me from her kitchen chair. "Hi, Carol. Kristine's giving me a perm." The room smells like bug spray. "Sorry about the smell."

Kristine takes up her station behind her mother and picks up the comb. "Mom keeps insisting on her same old stinky brand."

Did Miss Perfect just say stinky?

"It works fine for me, and it's cheap. You keep wanting me to get that expensive stuff."

"Oh, three dollars more a bottle! I'm sure we'd have to put

you in the poorhouse."

"Those three dollars add up, little missy."

Kristine snorts. "Oh, that's right, you grew up during the Great Depression."

"And don't you forget it. 'Use it up, wear it out, make it do, or do without.' That was our motto."

"And you walked five miles to school every day."

I smile at their bantering. "I'm just going to put your lunch in the refrigerator."

Kristine nods. "Good idea. Who could eat with this stinky smell?"

She did say stinky!

Ladora jumps into the battle. "Hey, no pain, no gain. At the end of this I'm going to look like a million bucks!"

"From which third-world country?" Kristine counters.

I turn from the refrigerator, holding my nose. "Well, you guys have a good day."

They both stare at me for a second, then burst out laughing.

"See, Carol knows how stinky it is."

I give Kristine a nod of agreement. "Yep, I'd pay the extra if I were you, Miss Ladora."

"Traitor!" Ladora throws a curler at me, and I'm out the door.

Next stop is Russell—the new guy. Actually he's been on the route for six weeks, but, compared with the old gang, he's the new guy. The entry procedure for Russell's place is knock once, wait five seconds, knock again, and wait until he answers the door. He's had back surgery and is going through extensive rehab. He's working hard to keep himself mobile, and door-answering is one of his exercises.

I hear his approaching shuffle, and soon the door opens. It's Santa Claus! Santa Claus without the beard, but, in every other way, I swear it's Mr. Kringle taking a break from the old toy factory.

"Hello, Russell"

"Come in." He's wearing a polo shirt and khaki pants, but he doesn't fool me. Look at that bright, cheery smile, those twinkling eyes, and that round little belly.

He tries to peek inside my basket. "What's on the menu for today?"

"Turkey goulash, rice, cooked carrots, and a banana."

Disappointment flickers on his face. "Oh. No cookies or pudding?"

"Sorry."

"Chocolate milk?"

See, he is Santa Claus!

"No. Sorry." I set out his lunch, wishing I could magically pull a carton of chocolate milk out of my pocket. "I do have an extra juice today, though."

"Really? That would be nice."

I begin to set out his food, trying to imagine a time when I couldn't just drive to the nearest grocery store and pick up anything I wanted, or, indeed, a time when I couldn't drive at all. One thing I do know is that I won't be one of those dangerous senior drivers that scare the wits out of me—those gray-haired wonders who don't ever signal and who make wide, sweeping turns from the far lane. I remember being totally shocked when

The Route

Janet told me about Goldie's final driving days. Sweet little sunshine Goldie had refused to give up driving well past the reasonable cutoff date. She could hardly see over the dashboard or hear horns honking at her, and the worst of it was that she decided the law concerning stop signs didn't apply to her anymore. She was in four accidents in less than a year. I vow to start making some attitude adjustments about my future.

Russell is opening his orange juice. "My daughter's coming to visit."

"Really? When?"

"Next week."

"How great. Where's she from again?"

North Pole.

"St. Louis."

"That's right, St. Louis. How long is she staying?"

"Three days with me, three with her mother."

Mrs. Claus.

"That'll be nice."

"Yeah. I wish she could stay longer, but she's got to get back to work."

Toy factory. "Lawyer, right?"

"Yeah. And she just got engaged. He's from back there."

"What's his name?"

"Ah, I think it's Ted. No. Maybe Nate."

I give Russell one of my mother looks. "Ooh, Russell. I think you'd better get that straight."

He chuckles. "Probably."

"I imagine your daughter will expect you to know the name of her fiancé."

"I might be in trouble?"

"Big trouble."

His eyes twinkle. "It's not like I haven't been in trouble before."

Santa on his own naughty list?

"I bet."

There's a knock at the door, and Russell shuffles to answer it. It's his rehab nurse, a stocky young man with a Marine haircut and with a tattoo of a scorpion on his arm.

Russell lets out a mock yelp. "Oh, no! It's my punisher!"

The young man smiles. "Exactly, so don't give me any guff."

I snatch up my basket. "I'll just be going now."

Russell glares at me. "Chicken."

"Well, who likes to see pain?" I answer sheepishly.

"Very funny."

I watch the nurse taking some weird instruments out of his sport bag. *Well, it is Halloween.* "Go easy on him, okay?"

The Punisher cracks his knuckles. "Only if he behaves."

Russell looks skyward. "I'm in trouble."

I sneak to the door. "I'll just let myself out."

"Okay. Hope to see you next time," Russell says with a grimace.

Leaving the Maple Leaf gang, I head for Lucille and Betty's. The clouds have turned an ominous gray and the temperature's dropped considerably. There's a smell of rain in the air, and I button my jacket all the way down and pull a pair of soft, black mittens out of my pocket.

I keep thinking about how quickly life has changed for

Maxine—how quickly it can change for any of us, and I find myself evaluating the kingpins of my life. Is my strength rooted in things of substance sufficient enough to endure such a punishing challenge?

And what of my compassion for the pain of others? I've just finished reading a book about the Buddha and the beginning of his spiritual journey. This man was a prince in India—a very pampered fellow. He had wealth, position, and power. His father didn't want him exposed to any of the coarse elements of life such as sickness, pain, or old age, so the prince was kept sequestered in the palace. Whenever the royal heir did leave the palace grounds, guards would go ahead of the caravan and move undesirables out of view. One day the prince decided to take a stroll among his people, and he ordered the caravan to stop. As he moved from the main road and into the side streets, he began to notice people suffering with all the natural consequences of life. The hungry, the sick, the elderly reached out to him. He heard their voices and saw their faces. His soul escaped the confinement of privilege and encompassed humanity. He gave up life in the palace to begin a great spiritual quest, which culminated in a forty-day fast, and enlightenment under a tree. I think the young man's enlightenment actually began as he walked those side streets and his heart learned compassion.

Heaven for a Buddhist is Nirvana, and Nirvana means the putting out of fire—the fire of greed and selfishness. If the first great truth of Buddhism is that life is suffering, then the way to heaven is to ease suffering. Even the small act of putting a meal on someone's table, and I hear the fire sputter. The simplicity of the truth overwhelms me.

I pull up in front of Lucille and Betty's house and wonder how much longer I have with them. I haven't seen Marv around for a long time, which must be a relief for Lucille. On the other hand, she probably misses someone to keep her company and shoulder part of the burden.

I knock and hear the dogs barking and a door closing.

Lucille calls out. "Just a minute!"

It takes her a long time to open the door, and when she does, she's in her nightgown—her hair loose and stringy around her face.

"Don't get too close. I'm sick," she says in a whisper.

"Have you been to the doctor?"

She wheezes, then glares at me. "Now, how am I gonna do that?"

I feel like a dope. "Sorry." I hand over the newspaper. "Don't you have any help, Lucille?"

"No. My older daughter lives in town, but hell would freeze over before she'd lift a finger. Says she hates her daddy. Well, does she hate her sister, too?"

A gust of Halloween wind tries to pull the screen door out of her hand. "Come in. It's too cold out there."

I take a big breath of the crisp, fresh air and step inside the room. Lucille closes the door behind me. I've only been in this room one other time, and that was briefly. Betty lies in her bed surrounded by toy animals. She pulls on the ears of a well-worn dog.

"Hi, Betty." I move to the side of her bed. Lucille looks intently at my face, probably trying to discern the sincerity of my greeting.

"Say hi, Betty. This is the lady who brings your lunch."

Betty's wobbly head turns slightly in my direction, and I'm fixed by a pair of brown eyes. I smile, but Betty only stares at me without any indication of recognition.

"She likes you."

"Really? How can you tell?"

"Blink."

"What?"

"Blink your eyes."

I do, and Betty blinks back. I blink again. Same response.

"Hey! Did you see that?" I look over at Lucille, who is nodding.

"Of course. She's a very smart girl, aren't you, baby? She was third highest in her class when she graduated from high school." A memory flickers across Lucille's face.

"What happened?"

"Don't know. A year later she started to go downhill. The pea-brained doctors are still trying to figure out what's wrong with her. Ten years ago they told me she was at death's door. Ten years." Lucille hands her daughter another toy, then turns to me. "I'll just take the basket and unload the stuff in the kitchen."

"Okay."

When Lucille leaves, I survey the small room and its life-chocking clutter. There are cases of energy drinks, boxes of special senior underwear, piles of clothing, newspapers, pharmaceutical containers, old fast-food bags and cups, dog-food cans, and cardboard boxes with mystery contents. Almost every inch of floor space is covered. Small pathways are the only way to maneuver through the jumble. I look up from the floor to find the walls just as cluttered. There are pictures, floral shadow boxes, family photos, a ceramic eagle, a couple of crosses, and, in all truthfulness, a black velvet painting of Elvis. The most prominent picture is a painting of Marv and Lucille in their younger days. It looks as though one of their children may have done it in a tenth-grade art class. I find it charming and heart wrenching. The two sit close to each other, holding hands and wearing hopeful expressions. Lucille has shiny, jet-black hair, pulled back in her usual braid. She wears a peasant blouse and a large turquoise necklace, while Marv looks very 1970's in his brown leisure suit and wide, striped tie, his face showing none of the spoil of alcohol.

Lucille returns from the kitchen. "Here's your basket."

"Thanks. That's a nice picture of you." I say simply.

She grunts. "Thirty years ago."

"Who did it?"

"My son, Ralph."

"Where does he live?"

"Don't know."

I stand still, not knowing what to say. No wonder she never smiles. I reach out to touch her arm and she pulls away.

"He's a bum. Drinker, just like his dad."

"I'm sorry."

"Nothing for you to be sorry about. I should have got rid of Marv when he wouldn't go to AA. Maybe Ralph would have had a chance."

Betty yelps and Lucille moves to her. "Oh, my girl wants her lunch."

The Route

I watch as Lucille takes her daughter's wobbly head in her hands and kisses her forehead. If one of the ways we get into heaven is selfless sacrifice, Lucille's going to be first in line.

I turn and navigate my way to the door. "I'll see you two next time." I move out onto the step, and Lucille follows me to the threshold.

"Stay warm."

"Thanks, Lucille."

The door closes and I turn my face into the cold wind.

Life is suffering.

What I don't understand is why some people have to deal with so much suffering. Are these weary wounded just not receiving the care and kindness they need because the rest of us aren't doing our jobs? Are we lost in television or computer games, caught up in money and material possessions, too busy with schemes and aggrandizement? I wonder what message the prophets, Buddha, the Man from Galilee, or Mohammed would bring to us in the twenty-first century? Probably the same message they preached thousands of years ago. The route hasn't changed, only the walkers.

Althia is the newest person on my route, having just celebrated her ninetieth birthday surrounded by family and friends. She was quick to show me her fancy celebration cards the first time I delivered her meal. Her charming brick cottage sits on a half-acre lot and is surrounded by mystical pine trees. Althia has lived here ever since she was a bride, and she has filled the shelves with books, and the curio cabinets with treasured bric-a-brac.

As I approach the small house, I envision Althia and her five children playing games of enchantment among the big stand of trees. Of course, the pines weren't as large sixty years ago, but I'm sure the adventurous imaginations of her eager wee ones conjured the forests of Narnia or Sherwood complete.

Althia reminds me of Joyce. She is bright, an avid reader, and she remembered my name from the very first delivery day.

She's hard of hearing, so I knock with great gusto and open her door. "Hello?"

"Hello, Carol! Come on in."

Althia is a slim, elegant woman with soft silver hair and vivid blue eyes, who has one of the brightest minds I've encountered in an older person. I imagine in her youth she stopped traffic with that combination—the brains of Eleanor Roosevelt and the drop-dead good looks of Lauren Bacall.

I move into the living room to find Althia sitting in her comfortable wing-back chair engaged in letter writing. Across her lap is a flat tray covered with stationery, envelopes, and stamps.

She beams up at me. "Please, come in. I'm up to my ears in correspondence."

I use my loud voice. "How long have you been at this?"

"All morning. My hand is beginning to cramp."

"Ouch."

"Would you mind setting my tray on the big table?"

"Be glad to." I lift the diminutive writing desk off her lap and deposit it in the dining room.

"Thank you so much." She flexes her right hand. "I was on the verge of carpel tunnel."

I chuckle at her doctor-like assessment.

The Route

"So, what's for lunch today?" she asks, trying to peek into the basket.

"Turkey goulash," I answer without much enthusiasm.

"Turkey goulash? You know, I don't think I've ever eaten turkey goulash. What an adventure! Ninety years old and eating something new. Isn't that remarkable?"

"Well, I wouldn't get too excited until you've tasted it."

She chuckles at my skeptical expression. "Perhaps there's a good reason I've gone ninety years without turkey goulash?"

"Could be."

She moves a stack of books on her side table so I can set out her lunch.

"New books?" I ask, already knowing the answer.

"My son just brought them over from the library yesterday. I'm reading the one about that young actor who has Parkinson's disease."

"Michael J. Fox?"

"Yes. Quite a story. I just love biographies and autobiographies. I've probably read the story of every famous person."

"Any idea how many books you've read, Althia?"

Her eyes widen. "In my lifetime?" I nod. "Heavens, I couldn't even guess. Thousands, I would imagine."

Thousands. No wonder she's so bright. I think about all those synapses sparking eagerly between the knowledge and information in her brain. I make a mental note to keep reading books until I'm ninety, even if I have to humble myself into bifocals.

"Well, I think that's everything."

Althia leans over and examines the food. "Hmm. I'll let you know how yummy it is."

I smile at the irony in her voice. "Okay, I'll see you next Thursday, and I'll bring a comment form."

"Bring two." She gives me a little wave. "Have a good day, Carol, and watch out for hobgoblins."

"I will."

I step out onto her porch and glance over to the magical arbor of pine trees. The moist air is heavy with their scent, and I long to walk within the cold shadows of their branches, returning to my childhood where I unflinchingly believed in talking forest animals, and fairies, and being able to fly.

Secured within the ring of trees is an inviting wooden bench. Oh, to be one of Althia's children, or grandchildren, sitting on that bench and listening to her read the wonders of Oz or Neverland or Mr. Toad. I can't help but feel that television and video games have robbed so many children of an enchanting oasis.

I reluctantly head for the SUV and the unpredictable happenings awaiting me at Elsie's condo. I don't know if I'll have Energetic Elsie for long, as she's eighty-two and suffering with dementia. Luckily, she has a caring daughter and son-in-law who are deciding where she should go and when. In my opinion, the "where" should be a supervised care facility, and the "when" should be soon.

The first time I went into Elsie's home, I smelled something burning and ran to the kitchen to find a blackened pot of oatmeal on the stove. (I think it was oatmeal.) The second time I found her standing in front of her bedroom closet putting on her outfit for the day. The only trouble was she was wearing two dresses with her slip over the top, plus a blouse, a sweater, and two hats.

I also discovered right away that when I'm near her, she wants to hold my hand.

"Are you Peggy's girl?"

"No. I'm Carol. I bring your lunch."

"When I was in grade school, my best friend was Cheryl. Is that you?"

"No, that's not me. I'm a different Carol."

"Oh, a different Cheryl. Of course." She won't let go of my hand. "Are you cleaning today?"

"No, just bringing your lunch."

"You know, I have such good neighbors."

"That's wonderful." I gently pull my hand away, but she immediately reaches for it.

"Are you Peggy's girl?"

"No, that's not me. Now, Elsie, I'm going to set your lunch on the table, okay?" I take several steps back, bringing my hand with me.

She smiles. "Did you bring my lunch?"

"I did." I move to her dining room table and she follows.

"My stove doesn't work anymore."

Of course it doesn't, because her son-in-law unplugged it.

I begin setting out the containers, and she watches every move. I smile at her. "Would you like me to open your milk?" I ask as I show her the carton.

"Yes, please. You know, I have such good neighbors."

"I know."

She reaches for my hand. "You do? Do you know my good neighbors?"

"Not really, but . . ."

"Why, you're Peggy's girl, aren't you?"

I sigh and give in. "That's right. Peggy's girl."

"Well, how nice you came to visit me. I haven't seen your mother in a long time."

"She sends her love."

Elsie beams. "How nice."

"I have to be going now, Elsie."

"All right, dear. Come again soon."

"How about next Thursday?"

"That would be lovely."

I retrieve my hand and move to the door. Elsie is carrying on a conversation with herself, so I forego my parting good-bye, as it would be rude to interrupt.

The fellowship I've shared over the months with these scrappy older folks has elevated my perspective on what I once considered to be the dastardly process of getting old. There is no sadness in being eighty or ninety. Advances in geriatric care and genetic research means a fair number of us will slip into those rumpled suits someday, and I've discovered that the key to being a satisfied senior is how we're treated once we get there. Senior discounts and parking spaces are wonderful perks, but respect and companionship are the necessities. It would be great to have children and friends around to help us when we get to the bottom of the ninth inning, but there are no guarantees. Perhaps, to hedge our bets, we should consider carefully how we treat people in the here and now as we walk the road of life. It's pretty reasonable to expect that if we're selfish grouches now, we're not going to magically transform into Mr. Nice Guy when the first AARP letter arrives. If we treat our children with respect and teach them to be thoughtful, contributing members of society, they will hopefully step up to the plate when their elderly parents need them. On the other hand, if they're overindulged, they get a nasty delusion of entitlement. They worry only about what's in it for them and how to manipulate their parents for the inheritance.

I pass by a couple of little witches on my way to Viola's, and the mimicry makes me chuckle. I've come to accept Viola on her own terms, simply because there are no other terms where she's concerned. From her sugary caustic remarks to her outlandish fashion sense, she is unique, and I've come to adore her.

As I round the corner onto Carnation Lane, I'm surprised to find her out on the stoop. The wind has picked up, and I can see her thin silver hair whipping around on the top of her head. Over her purple duster she's wearing a charming chenille bedspread, and for footwear she's chosen her lovely pink Keds. The look on Viola's face would make a lesser delivery person tuck tail and run, but I'm a hardened expert now. Then I remember I only have tepid turkey goulash and no dessert to offer today, and my aplomb flickers. Not to worry. I can take anything for a couple of minutes: nails on a chalkboard, thumb screws, Viola's soul-crunching scolding—bring it on!

I wave to her as I pull up, and her expression doesn't change. I jump out of the SUV and smile at her.

"Hi, Viola!"

"I called the office."

Not a surprise.

"Why are you so late?"

"I ran out of gas." What a whopper, but who cares as long as she buys it?

"Well, wasn't that a stupid thing to do."

Squish.

"Don't you look at your gage?"

"Of course, but I . . ."

"No sense, that's all there is to it."

Smack.

I nod. "Yep. You're probably right. Dumb as a fence post."

"Are you back-talking me?"

"No. I mean it. I should have stopped for gas. I just didn't want to be late." *Boy! I'm really getting into my own story.*

A cold gust of wind blows by, and we hunch into our respective coverups. I think Viola has the better deal in her bedspread.

"You young people just like to get the tank down to nothing."

Young people? Hey, it was worth the whole harangue just to be put in the young people category.

"So, where's my lunch?"

I jerk to attention. "Oh, sorry!" I put the items on the milk box, and Viola scrutinizes them like a restaurant inspector.

"Stone cold, I bet."

"Pretty much. I like your shoes."

"These old things?"

"The color's great."

The Route

"I like pink." She picks up the food tray with one hand and shoves open the trailer door with her foot.

"Do you want some help?" I ask, stepping forward.

"No!" she barks. "I'll do it in a couple of trips. You can go, because I'm gonna go eat."

"Okay. See you next time." I don't know if that's actually accurate, because if the meal office switches my route, Viola will be one of the ones I lose, along with Lucille and Betty.

As I climb into the SUV, I watch as Viola comes back out on the stoop to secure the last of her meal. She looks up and waves at me with the banana. I smile and wave back. *See? All bark and no bite.*

On the way back to the senior center, my mind wanders through the diverse struggles of my Thursday friends. Their hardships should have me feeling despondent, yet I find I have that same sense of balance I felt at Goldie's house. Life is life, and we have the choice to ignore, endure, influence, bemoan, or enlighten the process. Our choices make the route apparent.

Rain pelts the windshield, so I turn on the wipers. *Swish-swish, swish-swish.* It's like a mantra. I take a deep breath and enjoy the rain dancing on the roadway.

CHAPTER 9

The Well-Traveled Path

I am fifty... something, actually moving along to fifty-three, fifty-four, fifty-five, well, you get the idea. Old Father Time is a relentless taskmaster, urging us along life's road, unconcerned with our kicking and screaming, whining, or cheering. He just keeps us moving. How did that 1970's hippy song go? "Time keeps on slippin', slippin', slippin' into the future"? True enough.

Over the weeks and months with my Thursday gang, I have seen time's insistence met with nobility and humor, or fear and bewilderment. I have learned some practical wisdom on gold rings to reach for, and some dark pits to avoid. I have also learned that even the worst of life's collisions can be survived and conquered. The lessons often serve to teach—and sometimes to ennoble.

"Mary, how old were you when you were married?"
"Which time?"
"You've been married twice?"
"Nope. Three times."
"Really?"
"I know. Sad, ain't it?"

She sits making Thanksgiving decorations for the apartment's turkey-dinner extravaganza.

"What happened?" I hesitate. "Sorry, am I being nosey?"

Mary chuckles. "Of course not. Heck, most of this stuff happened so long ago, it's got cobwebs." She glues an orange construction paper feather onto the butt-end of a pinecone. "I was twelve when I got married the first time."

"Twelve?"

"Nope, sixteen, but I felt like I was twelve. His name was Richard, and his daddy owned the filling station in our town. Richard was the only high school boy who had a car to drive around. It was towards the end of the Depression, and not many people had cars, or gas to put in 'em."

She offers me some construction paper feathers. "Here. Want to glue some to his butt?"

"Sounds fun." Glancing at the lunch containers filled with ham and au gratin potatoes, figure I can take ten minutes to visit. I have a little extra time since Goldie wasn't on the list today. I'll be calling Janet later to find out the situation.

Mary hands me a pinecone. "Careful, they can poke your fingers."

I gingerly take the pinecone and start gluing.

She scrutinizes my technique for a moment, and then goes back to her story. "Where was I? Oh, yeah, Richard. Anyway, he was my first husband. He was seventeen. I was sixteen."

"That's young."

"Oh, way too young to be married. We liked each other okay, but nothing that was gonna last twenty or thirty years. When he turned eighteen, he went off to college, and we just sort of left off being together."

"Divorced?"

"Yep. There weren't any kids, so it was okay. When I

graduated from high school I moved two hundred miles to my Aunt Pauline's house to work in a factory that made pressed board. My uncle Hugh worked there before he died. He'd only been dead about a year, and my aunt was real lonely." Mary stops her story to inspect my turkey. "Put in a few more black for contrast."

"Will do." I have to smile at her dedication to the assignment.

"I lived with Aunt Pauline two years, then I met Cye—and that's C–Y–E, not S–I–G–H. Oh, he was cute and everything, just not a great person."

"Mean?"

"Sometimes, but mostly he was just stuck on himself. He liked me okay, 'cause we were married about twenty years. I didn't think I could have babies, but then I had Bill when I was thirty-nine. That same year, Cye took off with Vivian Perry."

"That's mean."

"Yeah. Cye and me weren't getting along too well then anyway." Mary picks up a piece of paper and waves it in my face. "Oh! Don't forget this red thing for under the chin." She inspects the butt feathers. "That looks good."

"Thanks. Go on," I encourage.

"Huh?"

"With the story."

"Oh. I raised up Bill by myself for the next ten years, then I met my Albert, the best man Heaven could have sent me. He was sixty, and I was forty-eight." She picks up a pinecone. "Want to do another one?"

"Sure."

She hands it over, along with more feathers. "Bill decided not to like Al from the start. Ouch! Dang!" She looks at me sheepishly. "Sorry, I didn't mean to yell like that."

I look up to see that she's poked her finger on a pinecone barb. I grimace. "Ow! Are you okay?"

"Sure. I'm tough. Anyway, it was just oil and water with those two. Not that Albert didn't try, but he was such a quiet man, and my boy just kind of walked all over him. Bill was turning out rowdy just like his dad."

Mary works silently for a moment, carefully placing each turkey feather in its colorful pattern. I marvel at the improvement in her eyesight since the operation. She still wears bifocals, but they actually look normal—nothing like the Mr. Magoo glasses she used to wear.

"Did they ever get along?" I prompt.

"Not really. Bill thought that rules were for other people. At thirteen, fourteen, he was ditching school and stealing stuff. Poor Albert thought it was all his fault. Heck, Bill had every chance to make good. Halfway through his senior year, he just took off—went to live with Cye and Vivian."

"How did that work out?"

"Didn't. They kept him for about five months, then some of their stuff went missing." Mary shakes her head and gathers up more paper feathers. "My boy was taught better than that." Her voice is husky with emotion. "I'm sure he was drinking by then, so everything got mixed up in his head. Dang drugs and alcohol. Sorry. I know your boy has some trouble with that stuff."

I nod. "Yep, but he's gone to a few AA meetings, so we're

hopeful."

"Hot dang! That's great, Carol." She looks at me with a little smile. "Bet you didn't give your parents a lick of trouble."

"Oh, I had my moments. I think we all have our moments."

"Ain't that the truth. Trick is not to get stuck in those moments."

"Amen."

Mary chuckles and sets her finished turkey on the cardboard tray. "Not bad, eh?"

"Looks good," I compliment. "Mine's a little lopsided."

"Doesn't matter. Half the folks at the dinner will think they're prairie dogs."

We laugh like fools.

A lot of people, when they think of God, see him as a serious purveyor of commandments. Mary and I see him as a loving father who gives us rules to keep us safe, and then places beauty and comedy along the rough road to keep us smiling. The key is to look up and see the beauty and comedy, and not just down at our feet trudging along the rough road.

I could sit here all day making turkeys and listening to stories, but there is insisting circumstance in the lunch baskets, and Viola at the end of the route. I finish my Thanksgiving poultry and place it in the tray.

I stand and stretch my back. "Well, I'd better be going."

"Okay, Miss Carol. I'll see you next Thursday. Thanks for your help."

"Will you tell me more of the story?"

"Part two coming up."

The Route

I smile. "You're amazing, Mary."

She looks up at me, startled, as though she hasn't been given a compliment in a long time.

"I mean it. You've been through a lot of tough stuff."

"Same as everybody else."

"I'm thinking a tad more."

She looks down and picks at the glue on her fingers. "Well, my daddy taught us kids not to bellyache. You manage the farm you've been given."

Basic wisdom.

I think of Tom's voyage from China, Bea's sojourn from wellness and privilege to lunches in a cardboard carton, Maxine's journey through cancer—all my Thursday gang on pilgrimages to that final significant destination. Each life important. Each life telling.

I continue on my route. Bea is at the hairdressers. Maxine is sleeping. Ladora is planning to go with a group of seniors on a trip to Branson, Missouri. Russell's back is hurting so he's not in the mood to visit.

Lucille and Betty are the same.

"Hey, Lucille. Here's your paper."

"What are we eating today?"

I report as I hand things over. "Ham, au gratin potatoes, mandarin oranges, peas, roll, and tapioca pudding."

"Hmm." She sets the food on the small bed against the wall. "Could you do me a favor?"

I hesitate a moment, considering the meal delivery rules. "Sure. What do you need?"

"A couple of letters to the post office."

"Just dropped off?"

"Well, if you could go inside. . . . They're important letters."

"Oh, sure. I can do that."

"I just don't trust 'em in my mailbox."

"I understand."

"You're sure it's no trouble?"

"No trouble."

"Okay, I'll go get 'em." She moves off into the dimness of the cluttered room, and I look over at Betty, who is watching a game show and pulling on the ears of her toy dog.

I see myself climbing some rugged mountain in Tibet to ask a wizened wise man the secret of this particular life lesson. The wise man shuffles over to an ancient cupboard, rummages around, and hands me a pair of hands. Weird.

Lucille returns with the letters, starts to give them to me, and then snatches them back.

"Oh, no! I don't have any stamps."

I take them from her. "It's okay. I have some in my wallet."

"You sure?"

"Of course."

"I'll give you a buck next Thursday."

"No problem." I glance at the letters—one is to Publishers Clearing House, and the other is to Ralph in California. Ralph: the missing son, the drinker, the artist. I'm stunned.

"You found Ralph?"

"My cousin sent me his address. Don't know if he'll answer."

"Lucille, this is great!"

"We'll see. Maybe he'll want to check on Betty."

I can tell she's trying hard to keep hope at bay. No high expectations for Lucille. She's been disappointed too many times. I, on the other hand, am the foolish optimist who's already planning a tearful reunion.

"It'll work out. I'll keep my fingers crossed."

A slight smile touches the corner of Lucille's mouth. "Thanks for taking the letters." She closes the door.

I place the letters in the lunch basket and head for the SUV, deciding to make a quick stop at the post office before I go to Althia's.

On the way, I'm caught by the irony of the two letters, wondering which one will pay off. I've been entrusted with dreams and hopes—one with real value.

At Althia's cottage, I find an envelope taped to her entryway door with my name beautifully penned on the front. I open it and read:

Dear Carol,
I have gone with my son and daughter-in-law for a
drive into the wilderness—there to soothe our souls.
I am sorry for any inconvenience this has caused you.
Fondly,
Althia

I fold the note and place it back into the envelope. It's worth a slight inconvenience to receive such an elegant expression. Somehow e-mailing isn't the same, and I wonder how long before we lose entirely the personal connection of putting pen to paper and scrolling out messages of mind and heart.

The day has been basically without incident until I arrive at Elsie's condo, where I hear yelling coming from inside the unit. There's Elsie's voice topped sporadically by a second yelping female and undercut by the rumble of male bass. Since no one is answering the door, I foolishly let myself in and am immediately in the middle of a maelstrom. At first I think it's a skirmish involving all three persons, but I quickly discover it's a fit Elsie is having all by herself, with the rest of us caught in the crossfire.

A shoe whizzes past my head.

"Yikes!"

A burly man with gray, curly hair dodges the other shoe. "Oh, sorry!" A couch pillow flies between us.

The female voice chips the air. "Mom! Stop this!"

A bunch of newspapers are tossed skyward as Elsie moves towards the kitchen.

"Thomas! Don't let her go in there! Stop her!"

A book hits Thomas in the arm.

"Ow! Elsie, please calm down," he yelps.

"I'll sic my dog on you."

"Mom, you don't have a dog."

Elsie heads for the china cabinet.

"Mom! No!"

I join the fray, stepping in front of the ammunition depot. Elsie strips the basket out of my hands and lobs it at her daughter. Food containers fly everywhere. Thomas tries to intercept the pass but misses.

"Dawn, look out!"

Dawn throws up her arms to protect her face, and the basket catches her in the stomach. She gasps and falls back into the recliner.

"Elsie, stop this! Now look what you've done!" Thomas moves to Dawn, who bursts into tears.

Elsie stands glaring at me, but seems to have run out of steam. She turns feebly to look at her daughter. "What's wrong with her?"

"Oh, Mom," Dawn sobs. She finds a tissue and blows her nose.

There's a moment of shocked silence, then Thomas moves to my basket and starts picking up the food containers. "Sorry about this."

I catch my breath. "Not a problem." I go to retrieve the pudding container and find it's the only unit that's detonated, spewing tapioca shrapnel all over the couch. "Oh, boy. Here's a mess." I have this odd impulse to laugh.

Before I can stop her, Elsie comes over and sits in the pudding.

Her daughter yells, "MOM!"

Elsie jumps. "What? What are you yelling about? You scared the life out of me."

Thomas growls. "Don't I wish."

I do a *Little Rascals* double take at Thomas, and we both start laughing.

Dawn looks shocked. "What? What are you two laughing about?"

"Sorry, honey, it's just that . . ." He breaks out again.

I take a deep breath and start to apologize to Dawn, when Elsie blurts out, "I'm hungry! When's lunch?"

Oh, man! There's no way I can gain control now. Here I am laughing myself to tears in front of Thomas, who's a complete stranger, and Dawn, whom I've only met once. Poor Dawn can't see the humor in the situation, and I feel bad that I can't have some equanimity and compassion at the moment.

Thomas moves to the kitchen. "I'll–I'll–I'll get . . . towel . . . wash up . . . mess."

Dawn stands and moves to her mother. "Come on, Mom. Let's go get you cleaned up." She gently lifts her mother from the couch.

"I'm hungry," Elsie growls.

"I know," Dawn answers tiredly. "The lunch lady is going to set out your lunch for you."

"That's Peggy's girl," Elsie says, pointing at me.

They pass by me on the way to the bathroom. Dawn has the face of one of those suffering medieval saints. "Sorry you had to get into the middle of this."

I have sobered back into sensibility. "It's okay. I'll just put her lunch on the table."

"Okay, thanks." Daughter and mother disappear into the bathroom just as Thomas comes out of the kitchen with a towel and bowl of sudsy water. He is struggling to regain his composure.

"Wow, I needed that. You gotta either laugh or cry in this situation, and I needed a good laugh."

"Sorry I joined in."

"Are you kidding? It was great. I needed a laughing partner.

Dawn takes it all way too serious." He dips the towel into the water and starts cleaning. "I don't blame her. It's really hard. Her mom used to be such a gentle soul. Sad."

"I can empathize. My mom went through some hard times."

He sets down the cleaning bowl and reaches out his hand. "I'm Thomas."

"I'm Carol. Nice to meet you."

"You come every week?"

"Thursdays."

"Oh, then this is your last delivery here. Mom's coming to stay with us for a few days, then she's going into the care center. That's what the hysterics were about."

"It's understandable."

"Is it?"

"Yeah. But they get used to it. Some even like it better."

"Really? Well, that's good to know. I've been feeling pretty bad about insisting."

"You shouldn't. You wouldn't want her to harm herself."

"That's true."

"Well, I'd better get going. Tell Dawn and Elsie good-bye for me."

"Will do." Thomas turns and walks me to the door. "Thanks."

"You're welcome."

"I'm glad you didn't receive any direct hits."

I chuckle. "Me too. Elsie has a pretty strong right arm."

Thomas smiles. "She does."

"Good luck."

"Thanks." He closes the door, and I move off down the walkway. I haven't known Elsie long, yet I'll miss her thinking I'm Peggy's girl, and having her show up for lunch in unmatched shoes, a slip, and a flowered hat—sometimes two hats. A skilled-care facility will be the best thing for her.

I often wonder if such a place wouldn't be the best thing for Miss Viola—a skilled-care facility where they have attitude-adjustment seminars. Perhaps a husband would settle her down.

As I drive to her trailer, I try to picture her married—Viola and Mr. Viola. I've never heard her say a word about a husband, yet she wears a worn silver wedding band, and her très chic belts are always men's ties. It's a mystery. If I were brave enough, I'd ask her.

I pull around the corner of Carnation Lane and spy her out on her stoop in a man's brown trench coat. *Oh, please let there be clothes underneath that thing!* Viola stares at me as I jump out of the vehicle and grab her lunch. Two lunches! I'd forgotten that Althia wasn't home, and I have an extra lunch. I'm feeling much more confident.

"Two lunches today, Miss Viola!"

"Good thing."

"And tapioca pudding!"

"Good thing."

"I like your coat."

"Don't be stupid. It belonged to Willard."

I come in her front gate. "Willard?"

"My dead husband."

"Ah." What a clever detective I am, and with that coat Viola could be Sam Spade. Viola's raspy little voice yanks me away from my mental amblings. "What's the matter with you?"

"Huh?" I stare at her, doe-eyed. "What do you mean?"

"Sometimes you just drift off. You have seizures or something?"

"No, just thinking about Willard."

"Well, don't waste your time. What's for lunch?"

"Ham, au gratin potatoes, peas, mandarin oranges, roll, and tapioca pudding."

"Hmm. They outdid themselves for once. Set it here on my milk box."

I've been doing this for a year, yet she still tells me every single week where to set her lunch. She must get a charge out of being the boss.

She glares up from the containers. "Anything else?"

"I love you, Viola."

"What?"

"I love you."

Her eyes narrow as she looks straight at me. "You do not. You're just the lunch person."

"I know, and I love you."

"You're madder than a March hare."

I'm sure I agree with her, because I would have bet a million bucks that the words *I love you* and *Viola* would never have come out of my mouth at the same time, but there they are, and I mean it. I suppose because of my service, something transforming happened. I do love her, and I'll miss her when she isn't around to make me feel like toilet paper on the bottom of someone's shoe.

She pokes me. "Are you having another fit?"

"No. It's just that . . ."

"I'm gonna go in and eat now."

"Okay."

She motions me away. "So don't hang around."

"Wouldn't think of it." I turn to leave. I'm almost to the fence when her voice stops me.

"Will you be here next Thursday?"

I turn back and smile. "I will."

"Okay." She gives me an odd look, then gathers some of the food and moves into her trailer. I open the gate and leave the cute little wolf in grandma's trench coat.

It's been a fairly mild autumn, but in the last few days a cold wind has picked up from the north, making me long for wool sweaters and hot tomato soup. As I move away from Viola's place, the last of the dry leaves set up a clatter, and I think of Turkey Day coming up, then Christmas, New Years, Valentine's. Life is filled with cycles and possibilities.

EPILOGUE

Heading Home

Goldie is still with us, but she sleeps most of the time. Janet worries, because when Miss Sunshine is awake, she often gets into trouble. One day when Janet had to pop over to the grocery store, Goldie decided to go out on her own and get the mail. She made it to the mailbox but didn't have the strength for the return trip. Luckily, a neighbor saw her clinging to the box and figured something was wrong. He came over and helped her back into the house. Janet is about to insist on a move for sweet little Goldie, whether she likes it or not.

I say prayers of gratitude every day for the blessing Goldie has been in my life—gratitude for all my Thursday friends. When I first started, I thought it was about feeding a few hungry seniors. But, of course, over the months I have learned differently. With them I have laughed and cried and learned.

Tom is alert and ever the gentleman, surrounded by his large extended family. He continues to spoil me with treats: strawberries, peaches, and candy. He also tells me that I should visit China someday. Perhaps I will.

Mary is into chumming around with her senior companion. She watches over Jonathan like a bulldog, monitors the political climate, and yells at the newsmakers on television.

Bea has gone to live with her daughter and son-in-law in their posh home on the east side. I envision her surrounded by her treasured antiques and memories. I wonder if she misses her cardboard container lunches.

Elegant Maxine died just before Thanksgiving. I attended her funeral, where Beth spoke and the organist played classical music. I see Maxine, young and vivacious, in her beautiful garden, chatting with Schubert and Chopin, and walking everywhere with William.

I have lost track of LaRue and Elaine, but I bumped into Margaret the other day and found out that Olea is doing great at "Buckingham Palace." She has several friends at the center, and is feeling so much better now she's taking less medication. She also gets a gentle massage every week, which costs extra and drives her two greedy daughters crazy.

Ladora went on a senior's bus trip to Branson, Missouri, and is planning a cruise to Alaska with Kristine and family.

Russell (Santa Claus) has moved to St. Louis (the North Pole) to be closer to his daughter (the elf) and the rest of his family (who all work in the toy factory). Maybe I'll catch a glimpse of him next Christmas Eve.

Althia continues to read and to amaze me. Her depleted hearing frustrates her because she would love to sit and chat—enjoying other people's stories and sharing a lifetime of significant experiences. Just in the short time I've known her, she's read over thirty books.

Elsie was moved into her care center kicking and screaming (literally), but Thomas sent a card to me via the senior center, reporting that she has since picked up a boyfriend and settled down considerably. Ah, the power of love.

Lucille, Betty, and Viola were taken off my route just

after Christmas, and I miss them. For several months I would periodically pop in around lunchtime just to say hi and see how they were doing, then life went a different direction and I lost track of them.

Just a few weeks ago I grabbed my camera and went over to take pictures. Lucille and Betty weren't home, so I took a picture of their little house, imagining all the while that Ralph had come to reacquaint himself with his mom and sister and find them a better place to live. Well, who else was going to do it? God doesn't just reach down with a magic wand and zap things to make them happen. If we want things better we need to use our heads, hearts, and hands and do the work ourselves.

I drove to Viola's, anticipating a unique Kodak moment, hoping she'd have on her floral duster, blue men's tie belt, and pink Keds. When I pulled around the corner of Carnation Lane, I had a shock. The sleek sand-dune Airstream was gone! Where it had once sat entrenched, there was nothing but a cement slab, several cement blocks, and the old metal stoop.

I pulled over to the side of the narrow lane and stared, my mind short-circuiting on the possibilities. How could crooks steal an entire trailer? Finally, I raised my camera and took a picture of the stoop. I walked around hoping to find the milk box, but it too had mysteriously disappeared.

Logic told me that Viola had died and that her niece had efficiently cleaned out the stuff, held a yard sale, and sold the well-used trailer for a minimal price. But then again, maybe the scrappy little fashion plate got itchy for the open road. Maybe she'd backed up a big four-wheel-drive truck to the hitch on her trailer, hooked it up, hollered good-bye to all her trailer-park cronies, and headed off for the Pokonos or the Grand Canyon.

Yep. I can imagine Miss Viola and Mr. Buffy hauling along Route 111 with the windows down, the wind whipping through Viola's silver hair, and Buffy's doggy ears flapping, as they cruise contentedly toward saffron horizons and starry nights.

Heaven.

Author Bio

Prior to writing novels, Gale Sears was a student of theater. She received a master's degree in theater arts from the University of Minnesota, and spent her years after graduation acting, directing, and writing plays.

Gale is fascinated by history and people's lives, which explains her interest in penning historical fiction, and stories of the human experience.

Gale lives in Salt Lake City, Utah, with her husband. She has two grown children, a wonderful group of friends, and always a dog underfoot.

Please visit Gale's website at www.galesears.com.